ROADHOUSE MYSTERY

Noelene Jenkinson

Chapter 1

Holly Duncan grudgingly reached out a hand to stop the bedside alarm in her cabin behind the Coach Roadhouse. Some mornings lately she found it hard to face the day.

Yet another anniversary, the fifth now, of her mother's disappearance in the district, had quietly arrived and slipped by. Although not unnoticed. Almost daily she wondered how much longer she should stay here in this country community working at the roadhouse. Hoping for word. Suspecting that, on the law of averages, if there was ever any news it would most likely be bad, not good. To how she would deal with that if the moment ever arrived, she had never given any thought. She craved an answer but also feared it.

After her feet found the floor and carried her to the bathroom, an invigorating shower washed away the cobwebs. Dressed in her waitress uniform of black shirt and trousers, Holly tied on the full blue roadhouse apron bearing her embroidered name and old stagecoach logo. Pulled on the comfortable sneakers that cared for her feet all day.

She bunched and wrapped her auburn hair in a light colourful scarf, pulled on her favourite long thick jacket, slung a carryall over her shoulder and, in quick strides, braved the pre-dawn chill in the walk across the yard to the private back roadhouse entrance.

Using her staff key, she let herself in, snapping on lights as she made her way down the hallways past the warren of storage and cold rooms, bathrooms and her boss Gracie's office.

Years of routine and her senses stirring led her into Sid's warm bustling kitchen. She inhaled the aromas of fresh baked bread, sweet treats and full breakfast preparations for which her other boss, the roadhouse cook, was renowned.

'Morning, Sid.' She gave him a quick side hug.

Brother and sister, Sid and Gracie Townsend, single middle aged children of hippy parents, for decades now had held the fort in their roadhouse kingdom. Five years ago, they had not only taken Holly in and given her a job, but almost instantly became her surrogate family. Their unconditional affection and support was offered from the first moment they met and learned her identity and circumstances.

With his back turned frying bacon and onions on the broad grill plate, toasting burger buns, cartons of eggs ready to one side, his flat cap perched over long grey hair pulled back in a tie at his nape, Sid raised two fingers in his usual greeting.

'Peace, Sunshine.'

'We could sure do with some sunny days,' Holly muttered. 'I'm ready for spring.'

She grabbed her usual loaded toasted sandwich wrapped and ready beside the grill. With her free arm, she slipped off her coat and bag and hung them on spare hooks in the pass-through servery alcove between kitchen and restaurant.

Reilly, their casual and only other male staff member at the moment, had already finished kitchen-hand duties for the morning rush alongside Sid. As she emerged into the restaurant, the young man was tidying shelves in the mini market at the far end of the roadhouse before manning the checkout. Holly tossed him a wave then made short work of her hot sandwich and a mug of tea.

A familiar station wagon, lights on in the dark, pulled up outside and disgorged its teen passenger. Moments later, a red-cheeked Georgia, blowing on her cold hands, joined her behind the counter. The youngest of the hospitality staff, she worked this one mid-week opening and one weekend shift.

'Hey kiddo. You catching the school bus at eight?'

'Yeah,' she groaned, making herself the usual hot chocolate.

Always unenthusiastic at the prospect of school, Holly grinned. 'Almost holidays then one more term and you're done.'

Georgia's expression cheered up at the thought. After finishing high school, none too soon everyone knew, the girl planned on taking a gap year with jobs already lined up as crew on private yachts up north in Queensland's tropical waters, at least for the summer.

If it ever arrived, Holly privately sighed. Always anxious for the dark days of winter to end.

For the next hour, the girls worked alongside each other making sandwiches and salad rolls. Filling the pie warmer with hot snacks, checking and restocking bag and takeaway supplies. Filling the hot water urns and firing up the barista machine.

Gracie breezed in from her back office, red-rimmed glasses perched on her nose, for one last sweeping glance of all tables and cleaning before opening at six. 'Looking good, ladies. If you're all set, are we good to go?'

Holly gave a thumbs up, Georgia nodded and Gracie opened up.

From the first day she had worked here, Holly's gaze continually flashed to the front doors as customers both arrived and left. As her work load allowed, she scanned indoors then stared out the front windows at busloads of passengers, long haul trucks and vehicles refuelling. Always interested in their drivers and occupants.

It had started out as an instinct, watching for middle aged women with red hair, always hoping. Over time, her reaction had become an ingrained habit and while she remained alert, her heart no longer jumped in shock if a resemblance caught her attention. But the instant realisation still hit hard when the person always turned out to be a stranger.

Although it always felt cruel waking so early, especially in winter, the breakfast and morning rush always passed quickly. Georgia's short shift ended and she was immediately replaced by farmer's wife, Alice, having brought her own children to catch the bus too, then working over the lunch hour and early afternoon until the kids all returned from school.

Holly took breaks whenever customers eased since she was on duty all day, then joined the other part-time regular, Sophie. With the roadhouse workforce all being locals and friends, everyone knew their families, remaining flexible about shifts and hours.

Keeping a keen eye on proceedings and movements from her CCTV monitors in the office, Gracie floated in and out helping when and where needed. Warmly greeting locals and regulars, pausing at tables to chat, always a smile and interest in all travellers who made the stop along a country highway.

Despite their own troubles, Holly and her co-workers soon learned to be patient listeners and unofficial counsellors to everyone from colourful characters, grey nomads and weary truckies. And first responders in emergencies which had brought Holly here in the first place.

It was late in the day when dusty local prospector, Benny Wade, made a rare appearance and ambled into the roadhouse. Being a solitary old figure and infrequent customer, his presence was therefore unusual and created attention.

Holly was busy taking a family order, only half aware of Benny's conversation with Sophie. Something about a mobile phone. Didn't seem particularly unusual.

People were always handing in lost property. Sophie disappeared out back and returned with Gracie.

When Holly finished serving, she caught Gracie's glimpse of concern in her direction. Frowning, Holly moved closer. 'Did you want me?'

Glancing toward Benny and what lay on the counter, she noticed a grubby mobile phone. Its condition didn't cause Holly's heart to lurch but although damaged, the recognisable cover certainly did. This was not a possession someone accidentally dropped but one that Benny would have found or dug up after waving over it with his detector. Out in the bush. Away from people.

Gracie placed a gentle restraining hand on Holly's arm. With a quick shake of her head, indicating caution, she suggested quietly, 'Perhaps we could go into my office Benny and I'll take down some details.'

'Sure.' He shuffled around the end of the counter and followed.

'Holly, do you have a moment, too?'

She tried to push away the rising sense of panic building in her chest and managed to reply calmly, 'Of course.' She turned to her workmate, smiling. 'Sophie could you manage here for a while? Shouldn't be long.'

The girl nodded, her expression

9

sympathetic. An unspoken air of tension settled among them. Most locals knew Holly's background. The fact that it seemed Benny had found the phone while out prospecting in the bush would not have passed notice, raising questions and unanswerable possibilities in every mind until they gathered more information.

In Gracie's office with the door closed, she asked, 'Benny, where did you find the phone exactly?'

The old man had removed his battered hat, now scrunched in his hands and scratched his head. 'Well now, couldn't be tellin' you that but I could show you. Ain't any roads much out there. Me old ute has cut a track through the grass like, so I could find it again. Not a place people ever go. Don't usually see anyone else out there and I been prospecting half me life. Be rare to see another soul. Whole area was declared a wildlife and nature reserve years ago.'

Holly wondered if that was less or more than five years before.

Gracie turned to her and asked carefully, 'Does this mean anything to you?'

The implication of her question was clear. Did Holly recognise it? Choked with alarm at the sight of it, she merely nodded. Her mother always kept her phone in a full leather cover. Like this one. Blue. Like this one. Slightly faded but still identifiable. Being a treated animal hide the material would take decades to break down so it probably wasn't so odd that it had been found in such reasonable condition.

Because it was potentially important evidence, the reality of this find, its meaning and consequences, together with a deeply protective instinct, finally kicked in. Holly groped for a chair in support, finding her voice again.

'I don't think we should touch this.'

Because Benny was rarely seen in public, living virtually as a hermit in a shack he had built himself on a few acres he owned out that way, Holly guessed he would neither know her identity and possible connection to this item nor understand the significance of his discovery. To have found the phone so deep in isolated bushland pointed to more than a coincidence.

One more clue would help even further and she had an idea. 'I'll be back in a moment,' she said suddenly and disappeared.

She returned with a zip lock bag and disposable gloves. Pulling on a pair, tricky because her hands were shaking, she hesitantly reached out and picked up the phone. So far no one had opened it.

She unsnapped the metal catch and flipped back the top cover. Not sure she should even be doing this, Holly had to know. She removed the phone from the cover and turned it over. Damn!

'It's the same make as the one belonging to my mother.' The recognition and anguish emerged in little more than a whisper.

Holly didn't need to explain further, just sent an appealing glance to Gracie who indicated she understood.

'Benny.' Holly turned to the humble bushman who may have triggered more than he knew with this apparently insignificant treasure. 'Do you mind coming with me to the police station in town about this phone? I wouldn't ask,' she swallowed over the lump in her throat, finding it hard to continue, 'except it may belong to someone I…knew.'

His hunched shoulders lifted into a shrug. 'If it helps.'

'It really would. I'll drive you in and bring you back. Can you come now?'

He nodded. Holly didn't fancy losing him if he disappeared back into the bush again but he seemed willing, his expression wrinkled and mystified but obliging.

Holly replaced the phone in its cover then slipped it into the zip lock bag. After grabbing her bag and coat, Benny followed her out the back of the roadhouse to her car. They barely spoke on the drive into Horsham.

Eventually, he murmured, 'Not good findin' the phone out there, eh?'

Holly shook her head.

'Sorry, lass.' His soft comment was edged with apology.

She almost crumbled. His quiet observation and old brain had ticked over and finally worked out a possible situation.

When they pulled up in front of the police station, Holly unclipped her seat belt but sat a moment. When she felt ready, they walked inside together.

'Is Ewan Holt in please?' he was the only name she knew from hearing Billie Gibbs talk about his involvement with the recent drug bust out at Reedy Lake. Fortunately he was on duty and available to see her because within minutes he appeared.

'Holly Duncan. I work out at the Coach Roadhouse on the highway.'

'How can I help?' He glanced between them.

'I'm sorry. This is Benny Wade, a local prospector.'

Ewan nodded toward him. 'Sir.'

Holly didn't know where to start, feeling exposed out here in public, having to explain the reason for their visit. 'Can we speak privately, please?'

'Of course.' He unlocked a door leading from the reception area and led them into a private interview room.

Where to begin? To his credit, Ewan was patient but there was really only one option. Get on with it. Holly drew the zip lock bag from her carryall and placed it on the table between them.

'Benny,' she half turned to him, 'found this out in the bush today. I'm afraid there's a strong chance it may have belonged to my mother.' After a pause, she explained, 'Lorraine Elizabeth Duncan who went missing five years ago about twenty minutes out the highway. She was last seen at the Coach Roadhouse on her way to the Daisy Cottage B&B nearby.'

Holly didn't know whether to be relieved or concerned when Ewan's attention sharpened, he rose from his seat, said, 'Wait here,' and left.

After that, events and procedures took place in rapid succession. Holly was escorted into another room, offered a cup of tea by a police woman, Sergeant Louise Casey, who sat with her and explained that Benny would be interviewed and provide a formal statement.

'Because you have firmly identified the phone,' she continued tactfully, 'and it was found in such a remote location, it does raise suspicions. It warrants us taking Benny out with a team to the exact spot where he found it.'

Holly understood what that meant and cringed at the thought. For five years she had longed for the tiniest clue about her mother's disappearance. The phone may mean something or not but now that the situation was rolling beyond her control, she needed to face any outcome. She wanted an answer and would endure anything to receive it.

'We'll need to get a digital forensic specialist up here from Melbourne,' Sergeant Casey added, 'to try and retrieve any information from the sim card or internal memory. I'm afraid that's going to mean waiting a day or two.'

Holly nodded, realising any lead or further information was going to take time and patience.

'I suggest you return to the roadhouse now until you hear from us. Ewan and I will be your contacts. Would you like me to accompany you?'

Holly shook her head.

'Are you sure? This must be a lot for you to process.'

'Yes. I'll manage.' A lie. Torn between hope and terror, she had no idea how she would cope. One moment at a time?

'Don't worry about Benny. We'll look

after him,' the Sergeant assured her as they walked out to the car.

Holly nodded and murmured her thanks, grateful to slide behind the wheel, shut the door and be alone.

As she left town and headed out the highway her thoughts were in chaos, jumping all over the place. Why would her mother's phone be out there in the middle of nowhere? Her mind couldn't face the logical answer. Was it even her mother's phone? Had she made a mistake in identification? She would know within days.

What had really happened that night? After stopping at the roadhouse, it seemed logical her mother left to check in to the B&B she had booked for the night. But the owner had been interviewed at the time and said she never arrived. Her fear was that the police would find more in the bush. If not, this would be a false alarm and she might never know.

All questions she had locked away to avoid facing reality. But the biggest unknown was why Rainey had driven north up this way that night, four hours from their home in Melbourne without telling Holly before she left and giving no reason. It was so unlike her mother.

They only had each other – a single mum and her daughter – and had always been close. It seemed impossible that

Rainey may have been in some kind of trouble. She rarely dated and the friendships usually didn't last. As though her mother never intended any man to get close or become serious.

Probing from Holly about her father drew the same response. *He was a good man. That's all you need to know.* How many times had she heard that reply? And any further attempt at conversation or an answer met a roadblock.

Holly always wondered if her father was so great, why didn't they marry? Or at the least, he could have stuck around to see if the relationship worked. Didn't he care enough to watch Holly grow up?

She had looked on her birth certificate but, of course, there was no father's name. In time, Holly had always hoped her mother might reveal his identity but now she would probably never know.

The roadhouse lights shone ahead. Holly slowed and turned in. Darkness had fallen on the short trip out but, for once, she barely noticed. Holly couldn't even remember flicking on the headlights. She usually found night driving scary since that was close to the time of day Rainey had disappeared.

Right now nothing seemed to matter anymore except news. Any news.

She was sure of one thing. She wasn't

going back to work tonight. She tapped off a text to Gracie with her apologies then retreated to her cabin and locked the door.

A plate of hot dinner arrived soon after. Gracie had knocked and called out, 'You okay?'

'I'm fine. Just need peace.'

'Don't let the food grow cold.'

'I won't.'

'Call if you need company.'

'I will.' Holly sighed and smiled to herself. Gracie was such a mother.

Finally, her footsteps receded and Holly was alone. She retrieved the meal, locked the door again and turned on the television with the sound low. Not really watching or concentrating. Knowing she must face work tomorrow and the next day and the day after that.

But tonight, she needed to brood.

Chapter 2

Next morning, Holly forced herself to get up and push through another work day in the roadhouse. She wondered if word had been *leaked* about the phone discovery or did she imagine the extra small considerations and glances from Sophie and Alice? No one said anything but Sid gave her a rare hug when she appeared first thing and Gracie breezed about the restaurant more than usual.

After the third visit out into the restaurant from her office within an hour, Holly quipped, 'Am I not doing my job?'

'Sleep okay?'

'I'm fine.'

All the same, it was heartwarming to know she had people around her who cared. If she had stayed in the city, Benny's find of the phone yesterday may have ended up shelved in the locked display cabinet of lost property and forgotten, with no one the wiser.

It was almost midday when a familiar big rig rolled into the roadhouse and parked. Holly's troubled mood lifted at the sight. Local truck driver, Tom Searle, hadn't called in for weeks. Must have been on a long haul job.

Just watching him climb down from his cab was a treat. Muscles straining through his tight black tee shirt and jeans, brown boots on feet that carried him in easy strides toward the restaurant. Although his sun browned face was half hidden by the brim of his black Akubra that she knew hid a crop of wavy dark hair, he was one heart stopping man.

As much as she felt a hum of attraction since Tom had become a regular customer over the past two years, Holly hid her interest. Although handsome and on the quiet side, he was a local man who had caught her eye. Which raised a problem. From day one since she moved here, she had been readily scooped into the roadhouse family, could have settled permanently, but always imagined she would move on. Perhaps back to the city. So she had no idea how long she might continue living and working in the country. Didn't seem wise to start a relationship if she left one day.

Now, with the hint of evidence of her mother's past presence in the area, all logical thought had been thrown into upheaval. And any future plans about her life's path impossible to predict. It all depended what the police retrieved from the phone, if anything, or even if it would definitely be identified as belonging to Rainey. Not to mention the frustrating mystery as to whether the bush search team might find anything else out there.

Holly sighed over the tailspin her life had taken since yesterday. She simply didn't have the energy for adding more to her emotional load. Right now, she was living in limbo and could only focus on one thing at a time. So kicking off any new friendship or relationship didn't make sense and was out of the question.

An older couple entered the roadhouse just before Tom. In fact, he stepped aside to let them pass. Since Holly was free she served the pair first.

Tom removed his hat, caught her eye from behind as he passed and gave a slight nod. 'Holly.'

She kept her smile neutral. 'Hey Tom.'

As she tried to concentrate on taking her double order, she noticed Sophie served him and crazily felt a twinge of disappointment. Annoyed with herself for still feeling this darn pull toward him.

They had only ever exchanged casual greetings or a brief exchange, like today. Surely if Tom considered her worthy of more attention, he would have done so by now. Unless he was shy. She doubted it. Not a sexy confident bloke like that. Then again, maybe that was an outward mask and he really had no idea his effect on women.

Yet she was forced to admit that even if he had asked her out, she may have refused. Her future in the district had always been on shaky ground and her thinking had been to avoid getting caught up in a friendship that may turn into something more when it was possible she felt the need to leave one day.

Besides, if she was honest, it stung a bit that Tom didn't consider her appealing enough to chat up or ask on a date. Maybe it was her uniform. Black wasn't exactly a happy or flattering colour even covered by her blue apron and the full rusty glory of her hair wrapped up in a bright scarf.

But the dark colour sure worked for Tom, making him look exciting, even dangerous, suggesting trouble.

Then again the sad truth could simply be that he felt no spark toward her and was just being friendly. If that was the case, bummer.

When Holly delivered the couple's order, she noticed Tom in his usual table against the far wall near the window. Maybe he was keeping an eye on his truck.

Although that seemed unlikely. Anybody tried to move that damn big thing without him sitting behind the wheel, locals would notice.

Feeling frustrated and unusually cheeky, she gave him a thumbs up when he caught her staring and, damn it if he didn't flash her a slow smile, and winked. Moving on, she slowly shook her head and, from somewhere deep inside her chest, a laugh bubbled to the surface. One very small moment of happiness in a long distracting day.

Later, Holly gathered the courage to ask Gracie about Tom. Even knowing her boss would leap to the wrong conclusion. All things considered, she had no good reason. She simply itched to know more about him. For sure it was a risk to be showing interest. Holly felt vulnerable enough at the moment and pulling up the courage to do anything scary was a risk.

From time to time, Reilly took over the kitchen of an evening while Holly joined Sid and Gracie for dinner in the restaurant. Tonight before she grabbed a meal and retreated to her cabin, she stopped at her boss' open office door.

'Need to ask you something.'

Gracie peered at her over the top of her red glasses, threw down her pen and sat back in her chair, arms crossed. 'Fire away.'

'No teasing.'

'Do I need to promise?'

'Try.'

Gracie chuckled. 'Do my best.'

'What's Tom Searle's background?'

Gracie raised her eyebrows in surprise. 'Son of local farmers. They run sheep south of the highway. As you know, it's good grazing country this side of the mountains. Lots of roos and emus, too, in the Wartook Valley.'

'Why has he only been around in recent years?'

'He was a FIFO worker in the Pilbara iron ore mines out west. A haul truck driver, I believe. You know those monsters where the wheels are taller than a person and the operator needs to climb a ladder to get up into the cab?'

Holly grinned. 'So, driving a B Double is a piece of cake then.'

'Something like that.'

'Interesting. Thanks.'

After eating dinner alone in her cabin by choice, which neither Sid nor Gracie questioned, needing the isolation after a busy working day and the wait for impending news, Holly tried to sleep with confused thoughts of Tom and the unearthed phone running through her head.

Early the following day, a police car pulled up outside the roadhouse.

Sergeant Ewan Holt and policewoman Louise Casey, stepped out and strode inside. They waited patiently until Holly finished serving a customer.

Gracie would have seen them arrive on the CCTV monitor and appeared in the restaurant. She glanced between Holly and the officers. 'You can use my office.'

Once they were all seated, Gracie closed the door.

'We've had success with the phone,' Ewan began.

Heart in her mouth, Holly waited for him to continue.

'We can confirm it's your mother's phone.' She nodded, unable to speak, suspecting what this meant.

'We've retrieved your mobile number and the texts that were sent to you after she left Melbourne. We've checked out the identity of some numbers but have drawn a blank on a few others. Do you recognise any of them?' Ewan handed her a sheet of paper.

Holly pulled her phone from her apron pocket and checking the list, scrolled through her contacts. None were a match. She shook her head. 'People my mother knew but I didn't.'

'We'll put a rush on the phone and keep digging,' Ewan said.

After the officers left, Holly found

working through the rest of the day beyond hard. She wanted answers but was afraid to face them. That night she sleep poorly and when she did manage to settle for a while, woke suddenly, as happened to her when she grew anxious, heart pounding, her head thick.

Feeling wretched by morning, she whipped off a text to Gracie that she couldn't face work and after breakfast, took off in her little red car. Having lived in the district for years now, she had become familiar with the local country roads and the different driving conditions. Some were sealed, some single lane with no lines and others unsealed. If they were graveled, it was fine but if not, dirt roads were dry weather only.

Today, preoccupied, she flew along a quiet straight stretch, not fully concentrating. She knew better but hurtled through a crossroad without a proper look both ways. Halfway across, she became aware of another vehicle approaching on her left. Luckily it must have been travelling slow enough to notice her and pull up in time to avoid a collision. Horrified at the near miss, Holly braked to slow and pulled over on the other side of the intersection.

A twin cab ute pulled up behind her and she closed her eyes, knowing she was about to get a piece of the other driver's mind.

She wound down her window. 'I'm so sorry-' came out of her mouth seconds before she recognised him. Holly moaned. Could her day get any worse? 'Tom. Hi.'

He assessed her. 'Not injured?' She shook her head. He frowned. 'You're not okay.' It wasn't a question, it wasn't about her physical wellbeing and blokes weren't always so perceptive. He opened her door and hunkered down at eye level. 'Take some deep breaths. You've had a shock.'

He had no idea but because of his kindness, she lost it and covered her face with her hands. 'I'm so sorry.'

'We're both fine. Don't be upset.'

Shaking her head, Holly braved a look at him. 'I'm not, about this.'

Tom pulled his lazy grin. She wondered if he had any idea how wickedly handsome that made him. 'I'm surprised this little machine goes so fast. You were really scooting along.'

'I'm so sorry. I've had a few bad days.'

'Sorry to hear it.'

'I shouldn't even be driving.'

He placed a hand over hers. 'You're trembling. Here have a sip of water.' He handed her a bottle and she took a gulp. 'You should step out and take a breather.'

Holly hoped her legs weren't as shaky as her hands but did as he suggested. Leaning against her car, she closed her eyes and did deep breathing. A light breeze brushed her face and played with tendrils of hair about her face. All she could think of was that she must look a mess. She had hastily dressed and rushed out of her cabin, wearing only pull-ons and a long sloppy tee shirt. She tugged her favourite jacket tighter around her.

By his slight movement beside her and the faint aroma of something woody and nice, Tom was close. She opened her eyes to see him lounging against her car, too, long legs stretched out, booted feet crossed at the ankles. Quiet and calm. Waiting.

In that moment, Holly wished she could bottle the sense of rapport and connection she felt to open and use another time. 'I'm sorry.'

Tom chuckled. 'Three times is enough. You're okay. That's the main thing.'

Holly drew in a shaky breath and said, 'Actually I'm not.' Pushed by some unknown compulsion and before she changed her mind, she added, 'Benny Wade found my mother's phone in bushland on the other side of the highway a few days ago when he was out prospecting. She went missing five years ago.' He probably already knew her circumstances. Most people did by now. Still, it seemed important to explain.

Tom didn't say a word but she felt him stiffen and he reached out a rough warm hand to rest on her arm. 'I believe I've heard.'

'Police identified it this morning. They're searching out there. Guess I'll hear if they find anything else.'

'Anything I can do,' he murmured, 'just holler.'

'Thanks.'

'You be okay? I can follow you back to the roadhouse.'

Holly shook her head. 'That's thoughtful. I'll be right in a minute.'

'Sure I can't drive you back? Drop off your car in a bit?'

'Really, there's no need.' She pushed herself away from the car. 'I know they'll find something. Just hope it's soon. The waiting, you know?' She shrugged. 'Thanks for the drink. I'm good to go now.' She was babbling.

'If you're sure.'

She nodded. 'Grateful I didn't hurt you back there. I owe you one.'

He grinned. 'Good to know. Can I name the favour?'

Surprised, she mumbled, 'If you want.'

'I surely do. Have an idea in mind

29

already.'

As Holly moved to get back into her car, Tom said, 'You can't leave yet.'

'Why not?'

He waved his mobile in the air. 'I don't have your number.'

'Why do you need it?'

'For when I call in that favour.'

She was about to mention he could reach her at the roadhouse but that might sound disinterested and mean. 'Okay. Sure.'

After they exchanged details, Holly realised that with Tom in her contacts, he was a step closer in her life. Did she want this? Once you got to know the guy better, he *was* irresistible. Amid everything else right now, she found that confusing. A complication she probably shouldn't encourage.

Holly climbed back into her car, feeling steadier now, turned around and waved as she drove away. Captivated by the man in her rear view mirror, with reservations. Tom stood in the middle of the road until she was out of sight.

It had been an effort to ignore Tom Searle for two years. After today's fateful encounter, she filled with the strangest sense that something had just happened.

Or begun. And the weight in her heart lifted just a little.

Chapter 3

Back at the roadhouse, Holly knew her light emotional high was short-lived when she noticed the police car. She headed straight for Gracie's office.

'I was about to call you,' her boss said as she entered.

Holly acknowledged them all with a nod but addressed Ewan Holt. 'You have news from the phone?'

'We believe we've recovered most data. It should prove useful in our investigations. We're working through everyone in her contacts. Most have already been identified as your mother's work colleagues or friends.'

'She didn't have many,' Holly said.

'No, and that's to our advantage.' Ewan said. 'One number is of particular interest. Your mother received many calls from that number in the week or so prior to the day she went missing,' Ewan continued, 'but they all went unanswered. That suggests she either missed them all but for some reason, didn't return them. Or she chose to ignore them.'

After all this time, Holly was finally seeing a picture of the last days before her mother's disappearance, and found it confronting to hear what was being revealed.

'This leads us to believe there was a questionable or, at the very least, an element of interest about the caller,' Ewan explained gently.

Holly appreciated his tactful approach. How many times had he done this before in similar situations, yet still remained so considerate and professional?

'We can't identify the person because they probably used a burner phone. Cheap mobiles for temporary use,' he explained. 'Often favoured for criminal activity. Trashed after a few calls. So the number's no longer in use. The person obviously didn't want to be tracked but wanted to keep in touch. In your mother's case, probably against her wishes. It appears she may have been trying to avoid them.'

Holly nodded, understanding. She could work out for herself what Ewan was implying. She rubbed her arms, almost afraid to ask. 'Have the ground search team found anything else?'

'We'll let you know immediately we identify anything significant.'

Ewan's pause before responding told her more than he was prepared to reveal.

'We realise it's hard, Holly,' Sergeant Casey said, 'but we just need you to sit tight and wait. When we know more, we'll be in touch.'

Frustrated, she nodded. The cloud of uncertainty and building stress since finding the phone weighed heavily on her. So far the police had kept a lid on the bush search. No media presence meant temporary peace. But based on the interest five years ago when publicity exploded onto television and in newspapers, Holly could imagine the frenzy if anything new and substantial was found. The ache inside her was real and unbearable.

There was a sinister backstory here casting a shadow over her mother's mysterious disappearance. She refused to think that her mother would have simply vanished and fled to escape or to go into hiding for any reason. Not without Holly or at least letting her know. That action alone was so out of character for her mother. Until the police found solid proof otherwise, Holly clung to a thin thread of hope. Either way, she faced the horrible truth that she must prepare herself for whatever was to come.

After the police officers left, Gracie and Holly shared a glance of mutual resignation.

'One step at a time, kiddo.' A gentle warning, well meant.

Holly nodded. 'I need to get back to work.'

In the circumstances, she wasn't surprised that Gracie didn't ask about her usual drive to clear her head after another nightmare. It would have taken more energy than she possessed at the moment anyway to explain the narrow escape with Tom out on the road. But for his quick action and evasion, the incident could have been much worse.

That evening in her cabin, Holly's mind was in turmoil as she sent out pleas for the sleep gods to at least stop another nightmare and grant her a half decent night's rest. Then her mobile rang. Tom. Even though she didn't feel like it, she almost welcomed the distraction, if only for a few minutes. Sitting alone with boring television in the background didn't quite cut it tonight. After hesitation, she answered the call but, before she could speak, he jumped right into conversation.

'Can you manage a long lunch tomorrow?'

Holly smiled. 'Possibly. Calling in your favour already?'

'Yep.'

'There's no rush.'

'Just making hay. Have another long haul contract in a few days.'

It surprised her to discover she was disappointed to hear it. 'Okay. Around midday. I'll warn Gracie.'

'She'll be a pushover.' She heard the humour in his voice.

'Usually.'

Having an outing with Tom, whatever he had in mind, raised Holly's spirits after a down day on a number of fronts. Her enthusiasm and anticipation was far more than she could have imagined. At least it gave her something to focus on other than the hovering menace in her head all the time. Although she knew a certain level of guilt for feeling this burst of relief and promise.

Which didn't seem so important the next day when noon brought the handsome vision of Tom Searle strolling into the roadhouse. Moleskins and a leather jacket today. And no Akubra hiding that dark wavy hair. Nice. Holly dropped her gaze, trying not to stare.

Sophie and Alice exchanged knowing grins and flickered their eyebrows as Holly removed her apron to grab a coat and bag from the alcove behind the counter.

'Stop it. I'm simply repaying a favour.'

'Sure.' Alice chuckled and turned to serve a customer.

'Well, he's too old for me,' Sophie sighed, 'but I think he's hot.'

A double-edged compliment. Warm with embarrassment at the unusual but friendly teasing, Holly was deeply aware Tom probably overheard some of her work mates' conversation.

'Hope you're hungry,' he greeted.

'It has been a while since breakfast.'

Dating, if that was what you called this jaunt, was a rare event in Holly's life. For what she once thought was good reason, backing away from any persistent admirers. Now she wondered if she should have been more adventurous, less guarded. Opened herself up to a little fun.

Not to say she hadn't almost given in to a tug of interest across the counter now and again when a bloke caught her eye or stirred her blood. But she never gave the temptation wings. She'd had offers. From down home farmers' sons to bad boys on motorbikes. She'd seem them all come through and stop at the Coach. Some were regulars. Some she never saw again.

Tom opened the door of his silver twin cab ute and she slid inside.

'Where are we going?' she asked as he clipped on his seatbelt and they started rolling.

'I know a special place off a sandy track.'

She should have known better than to ask. Country blokes didn't usually waste words. Sounded promising though. 'To be honest, I haven't done much driving around the district. My little two door isn't exactly made for dirt roads.'

'You were pushing it along yesterday,' he teased.

'Never going to live it down, am I?'

'If you can get time off, happy to take you exploring.'

Enticing. 'Maybe.'

Once they left the main road and headed into the country, Holly forced herself to relax. Spring wasn't far away. Golden wattle had started blooming thick through the bush. Perfect time for a picnic with stirring company. Yet deep down she still felt as though she wasn't entitled to enjoy it.

When they had been driving a while, she considered asking how much longer. Gracie had given her two hours for lunch. A treat, since her shifts usually meant a quick bite to eat and thirty minutes, especially on weekends or if a bus pulled up, disgorging its passengers who all expected to be served at once. After all the Townsends had done for her, willingly providing a roof over her head and a job, Holly's conscience wouldn't let her take advantage.

By coincidence, just then Tom slowed the ute. She loved the road sign as they turned onto little more than a sandy two-wheel track. 'Two Mile Lane. Cute. Who names these roads?'

'Locals probably suggest it. Council would take it on board and make the final decision.' He nodded ahead. 'Get a great view from up here.'

They stopped and piled out. From the ute tray, Tom loaded up Holly with rugs while he lugged a hamper and small esky. Wading through soft soil, she was grateful for sneakers. Tom unlatched a chain gate in the fence.

As soon as they emerged from the bush at the roadside and out into the open paddock, Holly gaped. 'Oh, wow. Magical.'

'Thought you'd appreciate it.'

She drooled over the scenery. Lush grasses underfoot, compliments of good seasonal rain. Private and peaceful. Sheltered from the frisky wind that still had an edge of winter bite. And, to crown it all, a perfect background view of the mountains. Their rocky ridges lit by early afternoon sunlight, bathed in the familiar purple blue haze of eucalyptus.

Holly rubbed her arms and noticed that while she was drinking in this pocket of nature, Tom had spread out the rugs, unpacked the hamper and made himself comfortable.

'Come and sit.' He patted the space beside him.

She settled, hugging her knees. 'I'm guessing this is private property?'

'Owner won't mind. Used to come here as kids with mates.' Tom raised the esky lid. 'Beer, wine or water?'

'Wine.'

He filled a colourful plastic picnic goblet and handed it to her. 'Dig in.'

'Where to start?'

Holly was impressed by the variety of salads and fruits, cheeses, thinly shaved meats and a savoury plaited loaf of fresh pull-apart bread. They filled their plates, she tapped her chardonnay against his stubby of beer and tucked in. Not much was said for a while, as though they were easing into each other's company.

Finally, Tom asked, 'So, how you doing? Since the phone,' he clarified.

'Ewan was at the roadhouse when I returned yesterday. They've picked up one particular number of interest but it's no longer in use. I feel so useless not being able to help them. As though I didn't really know my mother.'

'Phones are meant to be personal. Don't stress.'

'Unless it was simply random where Benny found the phone, I have this dreadful premonition they'll find more out where they're searching.'

'Always possible. If I wasn't leaving

tomorrow, I'd go out and help.'

'Kind of you to offer,' she murmured, holding her wine out for a refill, nibbling grapes and strawberries.

'I bet half the searchers are locals. They know the land. I considered doing it today but I figured you could probably use a distraction instead.'

Holly swallowed back a hit of emotions that welled up inside. Tom had planned much more than a simple favour.

'If they don't find anything more, I'll break,' she admitted. 'It's the not knowing.'

Already close, shoulders touching, Tom put an arm around her shoulder. Oddly, the silent calmness of his gesture didn't send her emotional but gave her comfort and strength. 'So you originally came from the city.'

Sneaky. Another diversion. Holly nodded. 'Just my mother and I. Never knew my father. Mum wouldn't talk about him. Was always evasive. Just said he was a good man and that was all I needed to know.'

'Ever think she might have been trying to protect you?'

'From what? If he was so great, why didn't she tell me more about him and who he was? A name. Anything. Now I'll never know.' Holly shrugged. 'Anyway, you can probably guess when I was born.

Mum always said I was the best Christmas present she ever had.'

'Did you work in hospitality down there, too?'

'Nope. Loved legal studies at high school. After I completed a paralegal diploma, my placement officer helped me get an internship with a city law firm. I didn't really want to practise law. More interested in research. Opens up more career pathways in banking, companies and government.' Holly paused. 'Since Mum's been gone, I feel lost, like an orphan. I have no idea who I am or where I belong.'

'Family is whoever you love. True belonging isn't so much knowing and certainly not changing who you are. It's simply *being* who you are.'

Wise words. 'You could have been a psychologist.'

'Just sounds like you're feeling vulnerable. And that's understandable. You know what, I'll bet any person that needed courage at some point in their life, was unsure. Found it hard to be brave. But I bet they'd also have serious regrets if they didn't at least try. To take risks, you're going to fall and fail and know heartbreak.'

As Holly listened, she assessed Tom. The guy was not only physically attractive and loaded with wisdom, he also conveyed a sense of trust and peace. She wondered whether he was born wise, or what had happened in his life to create the man he was today. Maybe, if she got to know him better, she might find out one day.

'You're so damn right. I'll take your counsel on board. Enough about me. Who's Tom Searle?'

He grinned and checked his watch. 'You need to get back yet?'

'Don't wimp out. The short version.'

Tom paused a moment. 'Parents have a property in the district. I come from a long line of sheep farmers.'

'You continuing the tradition?'

'Not really. I help out if needed but I prefer machinery. Worked up in the Pilbara out west for years as a FIFO driving the big dump trucks.'

'How on earth do you learn to drive those things? They're enormous.'

Tom chuckled low. 'Company provides a week's training in a simulator with theory work before you jump into the real thing with another driver. Spend your shift loading and unloading into hoppers. Ore's processed then carted on those endless trains to the coast for shipping out. Tough isolated work but good money if you don't spend it. I didn't. Built up a stake so I could buy my own place.'

Holly wondered where. She wanted to know more about him but was constantly nagged by doubt. Felt like she was juggling balls in the air right now, not knowing where any of them would land. Over her thoughts, Tom went on.

'Contract was two weeks on and two weeks off. Twelve hour shifts, seven days a week. Not much down time. Lived in an onsite village with meals, swimming pool and lots of facilities. Airfares can be part of your package. Came home sometimes. Others I went down to Perth or travelled. Whale watching in season off the coast. Searching for dinosaur footprints in the Kimberley. Asia sometimes.'

Holly sighed. 'I envy that you've expanded your horizons. I feel like I've been anchored.'

'Life goes in stages. Give it time. Change happens when it's right.'

'Well your mining life sounds amazing while it lasted.'

'Wasn't ever going to be a long term plan. Always intended coming back.'

'Country boy at heart,' she grinned.

'Absolutely. You plan on ever returning to the big smoke?'

Holly groaned. 'Have no idea. Time will tell.'

'Fair enough. Should we head back?'

They loaded their picnic supplies

into the ute again, standing close. Because the moment felt right, she gave him an impulsive hug, murmured, 'Thanks,' then quickly drew away.

She caught his surprise but his dark eyes told her he probably would have welcomed more. Another time maybe. He could so easily become a habit, adding to her troubled life right now.

When he dropped her back at the roadhouse, Holly said, 'Thanks again.'

'You're welcome. See you soon.'

No doubt she would. Then challenged herself. What happened to her rule of pushing back and not letting anyone in? Seems Tom Searle had broken through that barrier and she was a willing accomplice. While they briefly hugged earlier, she had caught his fresh outdoorsy scent. Felt the brush of his unshaven cheek against hers. As she walked into the restaurant, her body heated at the memory.

Distracted, she bumped into someone and focused. 'Sorry Alice.'

'Woolgathering? Lunch date that good, huh?'

As she shrugged off her coat and retied her apron, Holly ignored the teasing. Glancing into the kitchen, she asked, 'Why is Reilly cooking? Where's Sid?'

Alice hesitated. 'He went out to help

with the search.'

'Oh.' Holly had almost forgotten. For a while.

When Sid Townsend joined the ground search deep in the bush across the highway, he expected a large police presence. What shouldn't have surprised him was seeing so many local volunteers. He recognised almost everyone. Men and women alike. Bushmen, farmers, fellow prospectors like Benny, and detector dogs on leads. It was clear the police were concentrating all efforts on a particular sector.

After giving his name and details on arrival at the communications tent, he was swiftly given instructions and handed a pair of disposable gloves. Warned not to touch anything that might be evidence, take a photo or alert an official.

It was concentrated work looking, but if it helped bring closure to Holly, Sid would continue for as long as needed. The girl had suffered enough. He and Gracie had watched her closely every day since her arrival and decision to stay. Back in the tent, it had alarmed him to notice a number of bagged and labelled items for forensics already, tagged with bright tape, presumably all to be investigated. Some looked like scraps of clothing.

After a number of hours, with darkness falling on another cold late winter night, Sid stayed watchful of everything happening around him until the search was called off for the day.

Following a message that crackled over the radio, a disturbance over near the focus area had him frowning. Suddenly, more police activity converged. Murmurs drifted among the searching team. Something of interest had obviously been found.

With an empty sickness in the pit of his stomach, Sid forced himself forward a few steps. By spotlight, leaf mulch and soil were being carefully brushed away. Feeling as though he breached someone's privacy, and unable to watch further, he turned away. He was probably needed now back in the kitchen for the evening takeaway rush anyway.

With heavy feet, he stumbled back to his ute. He must have returned along the bush track, crossed the highway and driven home but, as he parked out the back of the roadhouse, he barely remembered.

Behind the closed doors of Gracie's office, Sid and his normally strong older sister agonized over the information he conveyed. But until official notification was forthcoming, they could only wait. Both agreed, not a whisper to Holly. If there was any relevant news, it would be delivered soon enough.

Chapter 4

Before she left the restaurant for the evening, Holly stopped by the kitchen. Sid was scrubbing more vigorously than usual. 'Thanks for taking part in the search today.'

He stopped and turned to face her. 'Half the district's out there, love.'

Holly clenched her hands together. 'Does it look like they've found anything?'

'I reckon they'll let you know.'

'That's what Ewan said today. They know more than they're saying.'

'Don't get ahead of yourself, Sunshine. For sure, you have a problem in your life right now but can you do anything about it?'

She sighed. 'Of course not.'

'Then don't worry. It won't stop bad stuff from happening. It only stops you from enjoying the good. Didn't you have lunch with Tom today?'

'Smooth change of conversation, old man. You know I did. You probably prepared his hamper.' He raised his eyebrows in question. 'He's okay.'

Understatement.

'First in a while.'

'At the wrong time,' she moaned.

'Everything happens for a reason.'

Holly shrugged. 'Does it though?'

'If it means something to us it will become something. Try and stay in the sunshine, love.' He drew her close and kissed her forehead. 'Night.'

'Night.'

So much philosophy today, Holly thought as she wandered over to her cabin. If only she could apply it to the coming long dark hours of the night that lay ahead. All the wise words and reassurances didn't really help but she managed a few hours of interrupted sleep. Pacing her cabin in the small hours, making mugs of tea, then squeezing her eyes shut and willing herself back into oblivion. But no nightmare. Hopefully enough rest to make it through another working day. She did but, as with all her days lately, it dragged.

A new day dawned and Holly operated on automatic as usual, scarcely aware of what she was doing. Not really seeing customer faces. Fixing a smile to her own. Later in the afternoon, Sid went missing again from the kitchen to join the search, and returned. Tom was out on a highway somewhere behind the wheel of his rig. Then a familiar police car slid into a parking space outside. Ewan Holt and Louise Casey had returned.

By coincidence, Gracie appeared in the restaurant at the same time. Holly took in a deep breath and stilled.

'They just phoned,' her boss murmured. 'They want you to go into Horsham with them. They'll bring you back later.'

'Fine by me,' she muttered. 'I hate driving at night.' Based on their serious expressions, Holly figured that whatever the police were about to share was probably not good and going to take a while.

'Need company?' Gracie said quietly beside her.

Holly had no idea what she was about to face. 'I don't know.'

Ewan reached the counter first, Louise close behind. 'Gracie told you why we're here?'

She nodded. 'You found something?'

'Best wait until we're in town.'

Holly glanced down at her boss. 'Company might be good.'

'Sure, and before you ask, Georgia's mum is driving her over as we speak to cover the evening shift.'

The drive into town in the back of the police car beside Gracie was a blur. As they followed the officers into a private room at the station, Holly wondered if there was always this buzz about the place, with uniforms and plain clothes officers everywhere.

Once seated, Ewan produced a number of bagged items and spread them out on the table. 'These were all recovered from the search area within a reasonable vicinity of where Benny found your mother's phone.'

Holly hardly dared look but managed. As she let her gaze wander over what looked like scraps of clothing, vague recognition of some of the tattered material hit her hard.

'From your DNA,' Ewan began softly, 'on most pieces we already have a match with your mother.'

Holly gripped her hands in her lap so tight, the nails bit into her skin. 'I don't know what mum was wearing the day she left and … disappeared but some of these patterns look familiar.' She pointed out two. 'I remember these. I'm surprised they've survived,' she whispered.

Louise leant forward to explain. 'Natural fibres like denim and cotton and wool break down more quickly. These materials are synthetic. They survive for decades.'

'We have forensics working around the clock to get all our findings identified,' Ewan said.

Holly looked directly at him. 'What else?'

He folded his hands on the table. 'Are you ready?'

She nodded and felt Gracie's hand settle gently on her arm.

'We've also found … remains. We believe they're human. First we need identification,' he warned, 'but since they were found in a shallow grave near everything else we recovered, you should prepare yourself.'

Heart pounding and speechless at the unspeakable news, she nodded and reached for her glass of water. A stiff drink would go down better.

'Forensics will conduct an autopsy which will give us confirmation and more details.'

All Holly could consider was why? Whoever it was. Why? No one deserved this. Not the victim. Not the family.

Ewan was speaking again. 'Obviously suspicious and unusual circumstances are in play here, so the criminal investigation unit becomes involved now. Do you understand?'

'Of course.' They were talking foul play and Holly ached at the thought.

'There's nothing definite yet but our search has become a recovery mission.' Ewan paused, watching her closely. 'Most disappearances like your mother are connected to somebody they know. Usually missing against their will. And females are more likely to be a victim.'

Holly's hand went to her throat. A friend not a stranger? Could this get any worse?

'You can't think of anyone?' Ewan asked.

Holly shook her head. 'I thought I knew all of her few closest workmates and friends. Like I said, Mum wasn't hugely outgoing and social.'

'If you think of anyone, let us know. Won't hurt to check out any person if you only have the slightest reservation. The smallest nugget of information may lead to something the original investigation missed. Doesn't suggest incompetence. The missing person's team at the time would have worked with everything available to them at the time.'

'Of course.'

'We'll go over the original case files, revisit any loopholes. See if all the alibis back then were as strong as they seemed at the time. We'll need to dig deep. A lot of legwork on computer in the office.' He grinned. 'But it might give us something further along.'

No pressure to leave the police station was ever hinted. It had been a gradual process over time having information revealed. Time that had dragged and become more of a nightmare than her sleep traumas. She and Gracie were offered cups of tea and sandwiches. Holly welcomed the hot drink, craving anything stronger that might obliterate and numb what she was feeling. She wasn't fussy. But she couldn't eat.

Filled with an eerie sense of calm after hoping for so long, a mantra repeated itself inside her head. *She's gone*. *It's over*. Her heart knew it but she wouldn't truly believe until someone said it out loud.

Some time later, feeling empty and lost, as Louise Casey drove Holly and Gracie back to the roadhouse, she still couldn't wrap her head around all the information she was given.

'I don't suppose you know how to get hold of some medicinal weed?' she murmured to Gracie.

'I'll pretend I didn't hear that,' Louise said.

Gracie chuckled. 'No love. Sid and I are a bit out of touch. He tried it back in the day but I never did. Living free was enough of a high for me. But you know I always have top French cognac on hand. So smooth it will slip down and you'll hardly notice. Knowing you and alcohol, it will probably put you to sleep.'

'Sounds like I should have been

drinking it for years then.'

As Sergeant Casey pulled the police car around the back of the roadhouse, closed now with only security lighting inside and out, Gracie said, 'You get into your PJs and I'll fetch our nightcap.'

'Who'll open in the morning?' Holly muttered as she climbed out.

'To be honest, love, I don't care. Sid and Sophie will manage. After that, the world can take care of itself.'

Somehow, Holly struggled out of her clothes, left them in a bundle on the floor and grabbed something to sleep in. Gracie let herself in and poured two generous splashes into rather fancy brandy balloons.

'Let's do it right, love.'

A whiff of it smelt heavenly but made Holly's eyes water. She was never much of a drinker but, under Gracie's wide influence and tutelage over the years, was growing to enjoy a glass or two of wine.

In a flash of memory, she recalled sitting on the deck of Reedy Lake cabin with Billie Gibbs a few months ago, combining lunch and wine with conversation. After that day, she felt like she had made a new friend and they kept in touch.

Holly's mind returned to the present

and she clinked glasses with Gracie. After knocking back a few gulps, she began feeling comfortably relaxed and silently begged for sleep.

'You don't have to stay,' she assured Gracie later.

'So, you drink my best spirits then dump me. Nah. I'll snuggle up here on your sofa. Don't want you to be alone.' She pulled a spare blanket around her and closed her eyes.

After a refill, Gracie went silent and Holly realised she had fallen asleep. So much for keeping her company. She was alone with her thoughts again and, to her amazement, not really sleepy. But what was new?

On impulse, sitting up in bed, she reached for her mobile and pressed a number she had never called before.

'This is a godawful time of night,' his deep voice rumbled on the other end. Such comments seemed his signature greeting as though they were already in the middle of a conversation.

'I've had a godawful day.'

There was a pause. 'Talk to me.'

She pressed the phone harder against her ear. He sounded so close. She imagined him on a long stretch of highway, dark beyond the reach of his headlights. 'They've found more.'

Silence fell between them. 'You

okay?'

'No,' she croaked and almost lost it but pulled herself together. 'Gracie's in my cabin leading me astray with some damn good brandy.'

'Is she listening?'

'Breathing heavily on the verge of snoring.'

He gave a low chuckle and she sighed with pleasure at the sound. 'Remnants of clothing. And bones.' She heard his intake of breath and soft curse. 'Nothing definite. Waiting now. Just wanted you to know.'

'Wish I was with you. Take care of yourself.'

'Trying.'

'Call any time. Road can get lonely.'

'I know the feeling.'

They hung up. Nothing more to be said. For whatever reason, above logical explanation, she and Tom had touched something in each other. The awareness had always been there yet suddenly and only recently flared into life.

Holly knew she was grounded more in reality and not really into any higher beliefs or purpose about life. But she questioned the coincidence of being drawn to Tom from a distance and then almost running into him – literally – at a country road intersection.

The irony of two things converging

was not lost on her. All the same, caught amid the uncertainty of her mother's loss, it had made her stop and think. Had this new friendship happened for a reason? Did it fit a need in her life right now? Instead of doubting the timing and sense of it, should she simply accept the situation and be open to what possibility it might bring?

Yawning over thoughts of Tom after such crushing news was another overwhelming mystery. All too hard to contemplate in the middle of the night. Holly slid lower, pulled up the doona and, after a while, mercifully found sleep.

When she woke and first opened her eyes, Holly forgot. But it only took a minute for realisation to set in again. Grace had already gone which meant she had slept soundly enough not to hear her boss leave.

In the following days, trapped between the dilemma of no definite word about her mother, yet welcoming the phone calls from Tom on his Queensland trip, Holly felt torn between pain and happiness.

When the police finally returned, Holly's heart skipped a beat in shock, as though their appearance was unexpected. But instead of pulling up out the front, the blue and white vehicle drove around the side of the roadhouse to the rear. For privacy, of course, which Holly appreciated.

She slowly removed her work apron, warning Alice and Sophie she was taking a break. Halfway down the passageway she met Gracie. They shared a glance but neither spoke. As they walked together out the back door, the officers were climbing from their car.

Inside her cabin, Ewan took charge and after barely a heartbeat, said directly, 'The remains we found have been forensically examined and identified as belonging to your mother, Lorraine Elizabeth Duncan.'

Holly's hands flew to her face. There they were. The words she had dreaded for years but needed to hear. Numb, she heard Ewan go on.

'As a missing person whose fate was unknown and with new evidence, her cold case will be reopened. Detectives will begin fresh investigations.'

Holly's mind and body raced with the finality of his news. She nodded.

'Forensics have established the cause of death as a blunt force trauma from a blow to her head resulting in fractures, probably from a hard object like a rock. All of which confirms our suspicions of a homicide.'

Holly gasped in horror.

'Being an unsolved major crime, it is not subject to a statute of limitations,' he said kindly. 'Being a homicide and not a natural death, this case will be reported to the coroner. They'll open an investigation and inquest. Might take weeks. We're sorry, Holly.'

'Thank you. Any possibility of a suspect?'

Ewan shook his head. 'The detectives will re-examine the archives and all material evidence gathered in the original investigation. We'll take advantage of any new technical methods that may have been developed in the intervening years since the initial event which may help. With all our new information, I can assure you we won't leave any stone unturned. We'll build a suspect profile and possible motives. Was it about power or superiority?'

To Holly it all sounded so clinical but she understood it needed to be done for success. 'Why, Ewan? Why?' she pleaded.

'That's a question which we can't always promise but, in time, hope to answer for you.' He paused. 'We'll need to have a long chat to you. Revisit everything from five years ago. Tomorrow or as soon as you feel up to it. Meanwhile, it may be a few weeks before we can release your mother's remains for burial.'

'Oh. I hadn't thought-'

'This will all take time, Holly. Contact us when you can come into the station.'

'Sure.' She rose as they did.

After the police left, Gracie lingered. 'Anything you need, love.'

'I don't know.'

Gracie gathered her into a long hug. 'I'm so sorry, love,' she murmured. 'What about company?'

'I feel empty and sick. Not about Mum's death. I guessed that. Its *how* she died, you know? I don't believe for one second my quiet-living mother ever did anything to hurt anyone.' Holly frowned. 'Because she never answered that one phone number with multiple calls, I'll bet she was being bullied for no good reason.'

'I'll duck back to the restaurant and see if the girls need help. Be back to check on you in a tick, okay?'

Holly nodded. Her body felt like a lead weight. Gracie had hardly closed the door when she sank onto her bed, grief welled up inside and her body began shaking with sobs. She curled into a ball on her bed and gave in. Much later, exhausted, troubled sleep finally came.

On waking, two sleeping tablets and a glass of water sat on her bedside table, together with a note saying dinner would be brought over soon.

Sitting on her bed, plate on her lap, Holly could only pick at the food. Thinking too much alone and feeling a growing anger slowly building, she filled with a cold and fierce hope that the police found whoever was responsible for criminally depriving Holly of her mother, to ensure justice was done. She refused to consider an option where the monster responsible for such a senseless brutal death was never put away.

Whatever the sentence, it would never be enough. Nothing would ever replace the wonderful woman who had raised her alone. How she endured and resolved the hatred in her heart right now was an issue for another time much further along her life's path.

Every day for years had been leading to this. She knew it. Was forced to confront and accept it. But how to deal with it every day from now on? There would be no more wondering. No more anniversaries to face, knowing. Only one looming question raised its ugly head.

Why had her mother been killed?

Unable to face people in the following days, Holly couldn't go into the restaurant. Figuring she should push through the shock and grinding grief, she phoned Ewan, arranging to drive into the police station.

Gracie objected but Holly shook her head. 'I need to get it done.'

In town, Holly was led into a private room with Ewan and Louise, then introduced to the lead detective on her mother's case, sitting in the background, listening in.

'Before we start, Holly, for your information this interview is being recorded and will be transcribed. We'll need to go over the time of your mother's disappearance. Bring out everything about her life and friends. We can't rule out any acquaintance or contact as a potential suspect. Don't feel anything you might remember or consider is too small or insignificant. It may well give us another lead to follow.

'The biggest challenge with cold cases is finding out who people *really* were back then.' Ewan shrugged. 'Memories can be untrustworthy. People lie or forget. It can be helpful to go through old photos to give a glimpse of the person's life and people around them.'

'I haven't really gone through Mum's photo albums. She had a few.'

'We would be looking for people photographed with your mother that you don't remember or recognise. We'll try to identify them and track them down.

Helps build an historical picture. The fact that she left all her personal belongings was grounds enough five years ago for believing as a missing person, she was in danger. Add to that the phone texts she sent indicating she intended to return and didn't. And, as far as you know, she had no issues, family or financial problems back then in her life she may have wanted to escape or avoid?'

Holly shook her head. 'Certainly not. She had money invested from the sale of Grandma Duncan's house and superannuation slowly growing because she'd been working full time all her life to support us. Until I started working in recent years, then I contributed to our household budget.'

'So,' Ewan consulted his folder of notes, 'you and your mother were renting an inner city apartment which you relinquished after three months when she was designated long-term missing.'

Holly nodded. 'I sold off our few pieces of furniture and packed up everything else that belonged to us. It was hard leaving my position at the law firm but I felt a strong pull to be near where Mum disappeared. Just in case, you know? Sid and Gracie gave me a job at the roadhouse and a rent reduction for the cabin.'

'Right. So, just a brief recap. Your

mother suddenly left the city without telling you. It wasn't until her first text late in the day after you returned that you realised she had left. Your mother wouldn't tell you where she was or why, and if she had a destination in mind or planned to meet someone. Only that she booked the Daisy Cottage B&B nearby but, after stopping at the roadhouse, never arrived. You reported her missing the next day when you stopped receiving any further communication with her.'

Holly nodded her agreement with Ewan's summary.

'As you know, we tracked your mother's last highway stop as the Coach Roadhouse. She was also captured on CCTV but no contact or sighting of her after that. Your mother didn't have a passport so we assumed she was still in the country.

'An extensive search was conducted in the area of the roadhouse in bushland both sides of the highway. Hospitals were checked. We interviewed all of your mother's work colleagues and friends. Our media coverage at the time was used to raise awareness and appeal for information but revealed nothing substantial.

'Three months on, we provided full profile information for your mother and uploaded it to the National Missing Persons register. By the way,' Ewan glanced across at Holly, 'we're compiling a statement for a media conference as soon as possible. After five years, we're hoping it will refresh the case in the public mind. This means her photograph will be out there again. All necessary to entice anyone to come forward. We'll keep your face and name out of it.'

'Thank you.'

'Forensics have other DNA from what we recovered. Just need to find a match. So far, nothing from the existing police database but a suspect is out there flying under the radar. He or she has just never been caught before. One bit of new information or a slip up and wrong move, and we're in with a chance. After the media exposure, it's always possible the person responsible will be drawn out and return to the area. Make a mistake.'

Holly released a sigh.

'It's not as hopeless as it sounds,' Ewan assured her. 'We have the best detectives on the case.'

She hoped so but fully understood with minimal new information or leads, the possibility of finding her mother's killer would not be easy.

Chapter 5

Through the floor to ceiling restaurant windows, Holly's gaze landed and held on the impressive man in black climbing down from his truck cabin.

At her first sight of him for almost a week in which so much distressing news had hit her hard, she wished it had been anywhere more private.

It wasn't until she actually saw him with unexpected surprise – she knew he was returning but not exactly when – that Holly was struck by how much she had missed him. Her face exploded into a smile and she couldn't wait for their first kiss. She knew it was coming and ached for it. That dream certainly wouldn't happen in a busy public roadhouse. Holly gauged that, like her, Tom preferred his personal moments quieter.

So they smiled at each other, their late night phone conversations strong in her mind. He winked while keeping their sparking attraction restrained – at least for now - as she took his meal order and coffee.

Across the restaurant a short time later, she watched him on his phone and immediately her own mobile buzzed in her apron pocket. He hadn't! As soon as she found a moment, she slipped it out and read his message.

Need to take the rig home. Text me when you're free?

She replied with a thumbs up emoji and *Cabin 1 around 10*.

The fact they were unavailable to each other right now made his return even more appealing and shone a beam of light into her mood after the succession of recent dark days.

Sophie's mother arrived to collect her daughter early so, clock watching and with only a few last lingering customers in the restaurant, Holly hinted to Gracie she was punching out early and would she mind closing.

'Course not. You've had a tough week.'

'Thanks,' Holly murmured, wishing both her bosses a hasty goodnight on the way out before she dashed off to her cabin, darting glances about making sure Tom hadn't arrived yet. Every time they met, she was in her work clothes and although tonight was a casual meeting, not a date, she planned to change.

Holly pulled out jeans and a long black knit top, brushing her hair down.

She didn't feel like makeup so just spread a warm shade of gloss over her lips, hoping it might be worn off sooner rather than later. The cabin was cosy so she didn't bother with shoes.

When she heard his ute rumble to a stop outside, then footsteps and a knock, her heart pounded. This was crazy. She was a grown woman reacting like a teenager. Clearly her love life had been non-existent in recent years and the lightness of heart she felt hearing his voice and in his company signaled flirtation with a new romance, but she also knew she could trust and needed this man equally for support.

He leant against the wall, hair damp and wavy, legs molded in jeans, holding a decent thick bunch of golden wattle in one hand and a six pack of beer in the other. His rather trendy-looking fitted sweater pushed up to the elbows was a surprise. He could pass for a fashion model and obviously didn't feel the cold.

'Hi.' He held out the wildflowers. 'Fresh from a roadside near you.'

Holly took them, grinning. 'Thanks. That's sweet.'

'Was hoping it might earn me a kiss,' he drawled.

Ah. So that was his challenge. Leaving it up to her. She leant forward, inhaled the scent of him and brushed her lips against his cool, roughly unshaven cheek. She would leave him to make a move and kiss her properly later.

Holly set the wattle in a jug of water, Tom opened a beer and they settled on her sofa.

'Cabin's roomier than it looks from outside.'

'I thought it would be temporary but it feels like my own place now even if it's not a home.'

'That a keepsake?' Tom nodded to the mantel clock, one arm behind her, a big warm hand resting comfortably on her shoulder.

'It belonged to Mum. She inherited it from her parents. Grandma's side of the family I think.' Holly sighed. 'I should have asked more questions.'

'Your mother was a beauty like you,' he said softly, his gaze settled on Rainey's framed photo.

'Charmer.'

'It's true. You dress up just a little and, damn, you raised the bar.'

The hand that was on her shoulder drifted up into her hair and slowly massaged. Holly almost forgot to breathe.

'You're looking slightly hot yourself.'

As he leaned closer, their noses touched and slid sideways so their lips could meet. His were cool with the lingering tang of malt, exciting her body. This happening was real and strong. With a man Holly had silently admired for far too long. If she had known this thrilling electricity was waiting, she would have grabbed her courage and stepped up sooner.

When they finished exploring each other in every sensory way and drew apart a little, Holly said, 'It's my favourite actually. That photo of my mother. Maybe because it was taken not long before she went missing.'

He stole another kiss. 'You okay?'

'I'm fine.' That weary phrase rolled off her tongue so easily these days.

'If you're going to lie,' he drawled, humour edging his voice, 'you should tell your face first.'

Not much got past this guy. 'So wise,' she muttered.

'Out on the road alone and isolated, you learn to watch out for yourself. Read people and situations.'

'Okay then, so I'm getting there,' she admitted then paused. 'Ewan Holt said there'll be a media announcement soon. The entire country will know her name and see her face. I watched the news on the restaurant screen tonight but nothing yet. Maybe tomorrow. And that's going to open a whole new can of worms.

My life is just days of endless waiting again, for a different reason now.'

'Police have any leads at all?'

Holly shook her head and indicated a box on the floor across the room. 'They suggested I go through old photos so I fished out Mum's albums. See if I can identify other people Mum knew in her past. Haven't opened them yet. All my humble worldly possessions are stored in one of Sid's locked sheds out the back.' She sighed. 'They've found Mum,' she cracked a little, 'which is good and bad. And I know one day this will all be over, but, damn, I wish it was already.' She swiped at tears

Tom hauled her close against him. 'I guess you're not catching much sleep, huh?'

Overcome, she simply shook her head.

'I should go.' He eased away from her to stand.

'No!' She laid a hand on his arm. 'Hang around?'

When Tom hesitated and raised his eyebrows, Holly realized her message was mixed. 'I need you,' she whispered, 'but I don't mean sex.'

He chuckled. 'I don't expect it.'

'I hope you do one day,' she murmured without thinking.

'Damn sure I will. So, what *do* you need?'

'You could pour me a shot of brandy.'
'Your drug of choice at midnight?'
'Something like that.'

As Holly crawled onto the bed and backed up against the headboard, she watched Tom's hands, the way he moved. Easy and calm. Everything she needed right now. And maybe longer, but the future was too tangled to even contemplate. When he brought over her glass of amber drink clinking with ice cubes, Tom kicked off his boots and stretched out alongside.

They talked a while as she sipped and grew comfortable. Sliding lower, her head leaning against his shoulder, she didn't remember sinking into oblivion, just knew the man beside her was warm and reassuring when she nestled close.

She must have stirred during the night because when she woke, her arm spread across Tom's chest which rose and fell gently in sleep. Holly carefully raised herself to check him out, his face turned toward her, dark eyelashes resting on suntanned skin, mouth closed and desirable. God, he was handsome. She couldn't believe he had stayed all night. Even though it wasn't yet morning. Still that hour between night and day. Neither one thing nor the other.

She eased herself from bed, pulling on thick socks and wrapping her long jacket about her. She fingered her tangled hair to straighten it then stepped outside.

Holly loved this time of day. So peaceful, even the birds hadn't stirred yet. It usually meant work and heading over to the roadhouse. She watched the sky gradually lighten between the branches of gum leaves all around in the bush. Had almost forgotten what it was like to live in a city. This country was real and earthy life at its best, crisply pure. Especially in this pristine air. It did your soul good to simply *be* and enjoy it. She reminded herself to soak it up more often. But today her heart ached for her loss. Her usual full appreciation for nature was reduced and must wait.

Hearing her cabin door softly click and movement behind, she felt a pair of big warm arms wrap around her.

'Thought you said you couldn't sleep?' he murmured, his breath warm against her ear.

'One of my better nights,' she admitted.

'I'd have to agree. Nothing like a warm woman beside you. Not sure I wanna leave,' he drew away, rattling the ute keys in his hand.

'Don't tell me you'll miss me?' Holly teased, turning to face him.

He kissed her. 'Take care of yourself. Not that I care.' He backed off toward the ute, pulling a sexy smile.

More sure of herself around him now, Holly barked out a short laugh that echoed in the stillness around them. 'You're mean.'

'I'll make amends next time.'

'And I'll hold you to it.'

As the man climbed into his ute and fired the engine into life, Holly reflected on the wisdom of this friendship at this time in her life so filled with chaos and uncertainty. But she couldn't regret a moment they had shared so far and anticipated heaps more. Tom Searle, she believed, who filled her with courage, the first man to ever make her feel treasured and steal her heart, was worth the risk.

Although the authorities had managed to withhold the wider public discovery of Lorraine Duncan's body for a time, within hours of the police media statement revealing her identity, triggered by Benny's recent discovery of the phone, news vehicles arrived at the roadhouse, disgorging reporters, cameramen and crews.

Gracie was forced to stock up on supplies and hire extra staff at short notice. Every cabin was booked out.

In agreement with her boss, Holly was

moved from the restaurant to the mini market checkout further away from most crowds even though her connection to the victim was kept private and never revealed. This freed Reilly to work alongside Sid in the kitchen.

Staring out the front roadhouse windows in quiet moments at the swarm outside, Holly knew the sudden surge of strangers were only doing their job but, standing on the other side of the fence, could only consider them all heartless vultures. All the same, if it drew answers and a culprit for the horrific crime, she would endure. Whatever the reason, it would never be enough or acceptable. She needed justice.

Each time her mother's photo appeared on a television screen or in social media, Holly's heart twisted and she died a little inside. For her own sanity, it didn't take long before she stopped watching. She had always believed her mother would never have just left. Always believed her disappearance was beyond mysterious. Had reeked of suspicion.

A deep instinct had pulled Holly here to the Wimmera and the roadhouse where her mother went missing, always hoping one day she would be found. But, until now when the truth was revealed, she was finally forced to own and accept the reality.

Everyone at the roadhouse and locals alike took a deep breath while the frenzy lasted over the coming days. Holly prayed another breaking story erupted somewhere soon to claim their attention so she was spared this nightmare.

So far, all the publicity had not drawn one single new lead. Widespread and rampant speculation rumbled about possible motives and suspects.

Was it a former partner or lover? Alleged motives for homicide offenders was finely dissected. The primary factor that had led to the fateful event in Rainey Duncan's life. Holly learned that female victims were most likely to have been killed in a domestic argument or relationship breakdown.

She was stunned by the wild theories which in her mind only served to heighten the importance of other males in her mother's life. Making her dive deep once again into memories of who her father could be and was he involved?

It was important not only to Holly but also the police to dig deeper. When privately questioned by Ewan Holt or the lead detective on the reopened case, she grew frustrated, unable to offer any names or knowledge to help their fresh investigation. She questioned whether she had even really known her mother.

Had Rainey avoided speaking or

involving herself in few relationships to protect Holly or because she hid another possible side to her life about which her daughter remained ignorant?

Maybe one of the photos in her mother's album held a clue? But even so, how would she know? She didn't know his name or what he looked like so she drew a blank on every front.

On the other hand, any man alive who knew Rainey would have an advantage. Did he know her mother had a daughter and her identity? Was *he* the father? Why had he never come forward? Guilt? Disinterest? Maybe it was a person who knew or was involved with Rainey at some point in her life but wasn't Holly's father?

The other main mystery in the whole case was that Rainey's vehicle had never been found. No parts traced to secondhand dealers. Nothing abandoned had matched so far. No burnt out wreck anywhere. Which, even five years ago during their initial investigation, had frustrated and puzzled detectives.

The only ultimate theory they offered was that it had been completely dismantled, destroyed or dumped. Possibly beneath deep water. Since district lakes and streams became shallow or dried up completely in summer, to dispose of a car would have meant driving the vehicle away from the area and scene of the crime. Would any perpetrator have risked detection? Probably did it at night.

With Holly's mind buzzing, only quiet moments with Tom or his daily phone calls checking in to see how she was handling the disruption, kept her sane. Then one evening, she received a surprise and welcome call, recognizing the number as it rang.

'Holly, its Billie Gibbs. Obviously I've heard the news. Please tell me I can come see you and give you a hug.'

Chapter 6

'Hey, girl.' Billie strode toward Holly at the roadhouse near her cabin and wrapped her in a long warm hug. 'Wish this meeting was in any other circumstances.'

'Thanks. It was great to get your call.'

Billie glanced around, a nostalgic gleam in her eyes. 'Only a few months ago I landed on your doorstep asking Gracie to hide me until *my* trouble blew over.'

'You were in danger during that big drug bust. A cabin was the perfect solution. So glad you and Noah Sutton escaped from it all safely.'

They loaded their picnic supplies into the boot of Billie's blue SUV.

'Gracie didn't mind you nicking off early?'

Holly smiled. 'Even though it's a mad house with the media crawling all over the place, she practically kicked me out the door. I've been training extra new staff all week and a constant roster of local women have volunteered as kitchen hands to help Sid. They're covered. You're a lifesaver. A chance to get away from here for a while.

'I've had reporters stick a microphone in my face and start digging with questions. I just tell them I only work here, have no comment and walk away. Fingers crossed but, so far, the press haven't got wind of the fact that I'm Lorraine Duncan's daughter. A miracle since we look so much alike. I'm surprised one of their sharper members haven't done their background research from five years ago and dug out my details.'

'So, where are we going?' Billie asked as they climbed into her car.

'Head around behind Sid's sheds and take the trail away from the roadhouse through the bush down toward the creek.'

'Sounds like they shouldn't find us,' Billie quipped as they bumped along a one-vehicle dirt back track.

'That's the idea. Peace and privacy.'

Billie glanced across at her friend as they drove. 'You've really nailed this living in the bush thing, haven't you?'

Holly sighed. 'My city days seem so long ago now it's almost like someone else lived them.'

'So, you gonna stick around?'

Holly knew she meant long term and shrugged. 'Who would know? I'm certainly drawn to this place but I'm staying until they find Mum's killer. After that-'

'I guess in a way Sid and Gracie have become your family.'

'For sure. They've been my backbone for years now. Working in the roadhouse, you get to know all the locals and regulars passing through.' She thought of one in particular that had made an impression lately. Holly pointed to their right. 'Take that track down to the water.'

Billie turned off and they wove through the trees, emerging onto an open sandy area. Old gums lined the bank, their curvy branches reaching down to the creek, reflections doubled in the water.

'Pretty spot,' Billie breathed.

'Sid comes down here to fish,' Holly said as they parked. 'Been bagging some respectable catches with good creek flows since winter rains.'

The girls hauled their picnic hamper, ground rug and wine cooler onto the grass near the creek edges. Facing west and the lowering sun between the eucalypts on the opposite side, it was mild and sheltered.

'Must ask Noah if he knows about this secret gem. He goes fishing every chance he gets. He takes me out onto Reedy Lake but, I mean, it's so damn boring just sitting in a boat for hours. But I get it. It's about the place and the sport. Worms, tossing out the line, getting a bite.' She shook her head and chuckled. 'Personally, I don't see the attraction but each to his own. And we get to hang out together.'

'Yeah, I think that's why Sid comes down here. Gives him a break from the kitchen and roadhouse maintenance. He and Gracie never stop. They could sell the place and retire but there's no way. They're such an entrenched part of the community, I doubt they'll ever leave. Might hand over management one day but they'll always live here and stay involved. In the middle of everything else happening around him, Sid offered to put this hamper together for us. Earned him a big hug from me,' Holly grinned, recalling her last picnic with Tom in a paddock overlooking the breathtaking landscape of the mountains. Sid had made their feast then, too.

'This is amazing.' Billie poured them each a wine and held up her glass. 'To answers and friends?'

'Absolutely.'

They nibbled on snacks, fruits, crackers and Sid's trademark freshly baked cheese and asparagus tarts.

As the sun lowered and shadows lengthened, Holly asked, 'So how's life with Noah on the farm?'

Her friend's face glowed. 'Taking the plunge and moving back to the country was the best move I ever made.'

'So no regrets then?'

'Absolutely not.' Billie reached out and rested a hand on Holly's arm. 'Okay if I talk about my mother?'

Holly understood and nodded, appreciating her friend's thoughtfulness in asking. She may have lost the most precious thing in her life but she had so many other people who had shown her unconditional support these past weeks. The worst time of her life since her mother's disappearance.

'Heather moved into the other small brick house on the property,' Billie was saying. 'She's separated from my father now. My sister Melanie, a lawyer as you know, is helping her with a simple divorce. Sad but life needs to move on for Mum. She endured too much over decades but finally made her choice and is so much happier.

'Get to see my sisters and their kids often when we can all fit it in-between working. I'm reasonably flexible. I'm working with a local accountancy firm now but can nip out for a family lunch. It's a treat to catch up with nieces and nephews. Noah's little Rosie comes to visit often in the holidays. We go for jaunts around the property on the motorbike. Camping out overnight somewhere. And fishing,' she groaned. 'We'll be shearing soon apparently as the weather grows milder. I'm told its endless cooking while it lasts. That'll test my skills. You should see this amazing big country range cooker Noah installed. Never thought of myself as a cook but I'm learning fast.'

'If you need any hints or lessons, ask Sid. He never turns anyone away when they ask for help, especially about food.'

'That's a thought. Will do. By the way, I've spoken to Addie Kendall recently. We went to school together. Lives back in the Wimmera now. Another city escapee. She sends her thoughts to you.'

'Thanks.'

'Do you know when you might have some kind of remembrance service for your mother?' Billie asked quietly.

'Her body can't be released just yet. Hopefully soon. I think I need to get that over.'

'I can imagine that's hard. Saying goodbye, no matter what the circumstances, is never easy.'

'Do you ever hear anything of Piper Thorne?'

'Yeah, occasionally through Addie. She and Ben are still travelling and working out of their motorhome along the east coast. I think she's waiting to hear about the plans for your mother, too. She'll be back for it.'

Holly was touched to hear it and looking forward to a girls' catch up even if it would be under difficult circumstances. And Tom would be by her side.

'I've received so many cards and flowers and messages from locals who knew Rainey was my mother. It's overwhelming. In a good way.'

Billie shuffled closer and threw an arm around Holly's shoulder. 'You got plenty of friends. Lean on us.'

'Thanks. I'm working on finding peace inside,' she laid a hand on her chest, 'especially since knowing the way Mum suffered. It will haunt me forever,' she admitted.

'If it all gets too much, reach out. Talk. Cry. Whatever it takes.'

'The pain and stress never stopped while Mum was missing. I felt so trapped. Couldn't move on, living every single day in a kind of foggy darkness. Even though I was living, underneath I was barely functioning. Felt guilty for wanting to live a normal life. Or at least as normal as it was ever likely to be.' Holly stared out over the water. 'The sense of loss was always there. The questions.

Sometimes I would forget for a while then it all came rushing back and I felt awful that I forgot.'

During that time, Holly knew her feelings had plunged between grief and angry resentment.

With sunset and darkness approaching, a chill settled in the air. The girls pulled on warm sweaters.

'What happy memories or special things do you remember about your mother?' Billie asked.

Holly reflected a moment, grateful for the diversion in their conversation. 'If you mean physical possessions and keepsakes, I don't have much. Apart from her precious photograph albums proving she existed, I only have an old mantel clock. Mum loved it so I would never part with it. I'm supposed to be going through the old photos for the police to see if any faces stir my memory.'

'What's stopping you?'

'If I'm honest, a niggle of fear I guess. But also if someone knew Mum when I was young, I probably won't remember. Seems pointless.'

'Might be nice reminiscing though.'

'You're right. I will definitely make a start tonight.'

'Well we're losing daylight anyway.' Billie rose and extended an arm to help Holly up. 'Let's pack up so you can get to it.'

Back at the roadhouse a short time later and watching Billie drive away, Holly agreed with her friend's encouragement. She needed to hustle, take the lid off the box of photo albums and see if she couldn't kick some memories out into the open to at least try and see if she could help her mother's case. Although she wasn't sure the activity would be a distraction or simply deepen her pain.

On her first mug of coffee, Holly methodically removed each individual photo and sorted them into the oldest photos going back to her mother's youth over 20 years ago. There were childhood photos for Rainey with her parents, Holly's grandparents. Holly remembered them both well although they were elderly while she was growing up.

Grandma and Grandpa, Len and Elsie Duncan, only had the one child, their daughter Lorraine, so there were a few of the small family group taken together. Ones of her mother alone, the black and white photos not revealing any hint of the auburn glory that was her mother's naturally wavy hair, that Holly had inherited.

No suggestion of her paternal heritage, so no resemblance that might help her in determining if any of the males over the years in photographs with her mother could have been a partner or lover. She had no idea who or where her father's family might be.

Then, by estimating Rainey's age over the years, in order of when she thought the subsequent photographs might have been taken since, Holly began piling small stacks she believed were more in the order of moving forward with her own age as she grew up.

As the number of photographs grew, the words *needle* and *haystack* sprang into her mind. How on earth was she supposed to make sense of her mother's life from the few photos where she appeared with people other than those few Holly recognised?

As she struggled in her lonely search, by now onto her second mug of coffee, her mobile pinged. Kneeling on the floor, she reached for it.

How you doing?

Wading through photographs.

Want company?

Silly question. *Yes.*

It took a good fifteen to twenty minutes before she heard the rumble of his ute motor pull up outside. Boots crunching, a light tap on the door then it was pushed ajar. 'You're unlocked.'

'Very observant.'

'Anyone could come in,' he gave a

mock frown as he closed it behind him.

'I was expecting you.'

He hunkered down beside her seated on the floor and leaned in for a kiss.

'You're freezing!' she said, cupping his face in her warm hands, feeling the rough dark growth of his shadow beard against her palms.

'Not much of a greeting for a guy you haven't seen in days.'

Holly chuckled. 'So, how's it going over at your parents' place?'

'Mainly starting to move the flocks into the more sheltered tree paddocks ready for shearing, and cleaning out the big shed. Shearing team have started arriving.' Tom glanced down at the scattered piles of photographs on the cabin floor. 'You've been busy, too.'

'I can thank Billie. She came over tonight for wine and a chat. Gave me a push to start looking through Mum's albums.'

'So, you ready to take a break or … need some distraction?' he hinted, grinning.

'I've barely started,' she moaned. 'While I'm on a roll, maybe help first. Distraction later.'

'Such restraint.' He tried to look wounded but failed. 'What can I do?'

'I know the old ones with my grandparents are too far back to be what the police are interested in and the right time frame. So now I'm working forward to see if Mum appears more often in photos with a particular man.' She reached over to a small stack and picked them up. 'There is a guy that appears a few times. This one.' Holly selected a few photos and spread them out. 'I've flipped over to the back and there's no name. Just the initials RP on one of the older ones but they're all definitely the same guy.' She shrugged. 'Could be anyone, of course but the thing is, he and Mum seem much younger in a few of them but older in others. What do you think?'

Tom took a closer look. 'Yeah, you're right. He's a good looking man. Tall, dark haired, classic handsome but it's definitely the same person.'

'I've been studying them for a while and if you keep looking long enough you get a vibe for what the people were like. The mood when the photo was taken. In the earlier ones, Mum has that soft smile she always had when she was quietly happy and content. They're both well dressed. I don't remember that dress she's wearing but he's in a suit more than once so maybe a more formal outing of some kind. And she seems to accept his arm around her waist or at least be comfortable with it.'

'Okay. So what are we getting at here?'

'Now look at these.' Holly chose a few others and spread those alongside the first group. 'They're taken many years later. Again, they seem to be more dressy social outings, maybe an event or dinner but Mum's not smiling. There's no arm around her. They're just standing together. Like she posed just to be polite. Her whole stance is different and that dress in this one,' she tapped her finger on the photograph, 'she wore that occasionally around the time she disappeared. I still have it in a chest of her clothes in Sid's shed. It came to mind there could be DNA on it but Mum was fussy with clothes and with a special dress like that one, she would have washed it even after only wearing it the once. Do you think I should mention it to Ewan?'

Tom shrugged. 'You have the man's initials, a picture and the dress. Might all be helpful.'

'If Mum was seeing this guy, she knew and socialised with him over a long time, probably 15 or 20 years. So you have to wonder how they met. Through work or some club or group. Yet I never met him. She never introduced him or brought him to our apartment. At least, not when I was around.'

92

Holly's frustration grew. 'There's no definite identity or connection as far as I know. It's so vague. He could be anyone. Or no one. Not even sure it's worth reporting to the police.'

Tom shrugged. 'Give them a look and let them make the decision. It's a long shot but his face might come up on their database. Any other men in the photos you feel are possibilities and appear with your mother more than once?'

'Yes, actually.' Holly brightened. 'Way back when she was really young. Probably about the time of the first photos with this RP guy but he's not in them and she's always in a large group. The members of that crowd are different people and keep appearing in photos together but not all of them at the same time, just in a combination of different groups. Looks like they were her favourite gang of friends. She's young and laughing, really happy.

'I've been looking close at all these, too, and probably misreading attachments and couples, but Mum was photographed next to one particular guy more often than any others. In these few.' Holly handed a group of photos to Tom but decided not to sway his opinion and mention her observations. 'Notice anything?'

He peered at them all for a while,

frowning. When he glanced up, he caught Holly watching him, quietly helping her. 'The sandy-haired one?'

She nodded, smiling. 'Yep, me too. But no names written on the back of any of them.'

'Could have been an early boyfriend.'

Holly moaned. 'Who would know? It's all just one big fat guess.'

'So when things start getting to you, a distraction's always a good idea,' he murmured, setting down the photos and drawing her close.

'You're sneaky,' she chuckled as she encouraged him to capture her attention and, just for a little while, allow herself to be taken away from the deeper complications of life.

Chapter 7

First thing in the morning, Holly decided she had nothing to lose by reporting her flimsy idea about the men in the photos to the police. She gathered them up and, with respectful care, sifted through the trunk of her mother's clothes to find the dress. Simply handling them again brought a catch to her throat. Pushing past the ache, Holly bundled the items for the police.

After another usual busy morning shift, she drove into Horsham and handed over her items.

Ewan and lead Detective Norton appeared interested if not fully enthusiastic. Like her, she imagined the thin hope was simply another remote chance that in all likelihood produced nothing. With no other evidence or clue, at least Holly knew she had thrown a meagre contribution into the ring.

Later that day, Ewan phoned, reporting no match from their database but thanked her for the effort.

'Don't be disheartened,' he said. 'This is a process. We'll find him.

Norton's getting the team onto comparing the people in the photos, especially the men, with everyone interviewed after your mother's disappearance.'

Marginally reassured, she went back to work in the restaurant. Where once she had scanned patrons for any likeness to her mother as they streamed through the roadhouse every day, now she found herself watching for any tall, dark and middle aged businessmen in suits, or handsome blondes of a similar age.

Her stares revealed nothing, of course, and while she would never give up hope, she also didn't expect to see a potential match. The odds of success were about the same as winning a lottery. Ridiculously slim to unlikely. Her mood swung between despondency and a dogged refusal to keep looking.

What she also didn't expect was to have her gaping returned. In quieter moments, all the girls kept an eye on tables that needed servicing, clearing away and cleaning after one customer, ready for the next.

As she moved around among them, Holly became aware of being closely scrutinised by a short man she had served earlier. At the time, he had given her the shivers. When their eyes accidentally met, he always looked down. And it happened more than once.

Holly couldn't explain her uneasy reaction, simply that, occasionally, some people looked downright creepy. She had encountered the type over the years. Maybe this one seemed disturbing because of the short hair at the sides almost shaved to the skin.

Alice and Sophie had shared their similar encounters, too, in the past. They had long ago agreed on a pact to alert each other which Holly did the moment she returned behind the counter again bearing a tray of dirty dishes on her way into Sid's kitchen.

Although Alice had already left for the after school run, when Holly pointed him out to Sophie, the girl agreed.

'With that haircut looks like he's in the army.'

Holly shook her head. 'Too old and chubby for that. Doesn't look the type really. Unless he has a desk job.'

They stayed watchful and Holly mentioned it to Gracie, until eventually the guy left. The moment he stepped outside, he lit a cigarette and smoked it while he was on the phone. He finished the call, flicked his cigarette butt onto the ground even though rubbish bins were nearby and shuffled toward the carpark.

Holly had a crazy detective moment. She felt like racing out to collect the butt for evidence. Then scolded herself for being paranoid and let the urge pass. Taking a deep breath and thinking sensibly, she knew he would have been captured and tracked on the CCTV both inside and out of the roadhouse. With Gracie already warned, she would have noted the time and movements of the guy while he was on site.

That night, for the first time in a while, Holly's nightmares returned. Sitting up in bed sweating, her heart racing, she considered phoning Tom. Simply hearing that calm deep voice was reassurance enough. But she decided against disturbing him. Shearing was a busy time. He needed sleep. Besides, she had never been a clinging vine and refused to start now. She had weathered every single day for years. She could do this.

So, instead, she poured a more than decent splash of brandy from the bottle Gracie had conveniently left in her cabin and sipped while practising steady breathing until she felt calmer. Eventually sliding beneath the doona again as the need for sleep slowly returned.

Next morning, Holly still felt unsettled as she dressed for work before dawn and strode across to the roadhouse by torchlight. But also felt a small sense of quiet achievement for having battled her demons and won. She thought she had recovered until she greeted Sid in the kitchen on the way through.

'Morning Sunshine.' As always, he held up his two finger peace sign with his back turned as he finished putting together her breakfast sandwich. Turning to hand it over, he frowned. 'You're hands are shaking.'

'Are they? It's freezing out there.'

'You sure?' he challenged, hands on hips.

'I may have had a moment last night,' Holly admitted, 'but I got through it.'

'Good girl. Keep working on finding that peace inside yourself and you'll have peace all round.'

'I know. It's hard when they look evil though.'

'You're safe here.'

'I thought so. After yesterday, it messes with your mind.'

Holly hung up her coat and bag, made a coffee and ate her breakfast. Sophie arrived with the first hint of light, Gracie prowled the restaurant before opening and another day began.

Still haunted by her encounter with the creepy guy yesterday, Holly did what she had always done. Operated on automatic. Smiling at customers, taking orders, making endless cups of tea and coffee. Checking and clearing empty tables. Not really noticing life happening around her but always subconsciously ready. For what, she never knew until it happened.

At first glance, the suit that approached the counter seemed like every other businessman. Well presented, polite. In her current preoccupied mindset, Holly didn't immediately rate him necessary of closer inspection. The beard was unusual though and threw her.

But when he smiled and with that neat slicked back dark hair, although with a few silver threads, her heart jolted in shock and she froze. But only for a moment. She gave herself a brisk mental shake. Couldn't be! Must be her imagination running wild, triggered by pouring through photos last night. It was a coincidence. Power of suggestion.

Her hands trembled but, with subtle deep breathing, she forced them to behave. Just because he looked similar to the man with her mother in the photos, didn't mean it was the same person. All the same, Holly sharpened her focus. Trying to appear normal and not stare, she finalised his order, took the man's cash and handed over his change.

Still, she would dig out the old photos tonight to consider and compare, probably laugh at her blind delusions. She would have left it go at that until the man half turned to leave then hesitated.

Accustomed to patrons changing their orders. Holly said, 'Did you want something else?'

More softly spoken than moments before, as if in confidence or not seeking to be overheard, he said, 'I'm sorry for your loss, my dear.'

Caught off guard because he clearly assumed he knew her identity and bothered by his overly familiar choice of words and tone, Holly's heart thumped.

Pretending ignorance, she said, 'Excuse me?'

'You're her daughter, aren't you?' When she stayed silent in shock, he added, 'You look so like the photo of the missing woman recently found.'

Numb, Holly managed, 'Goodness, do I?'

The tight fake smile he pulled terrified her. Either this man could be the one in the photo and actually knew and recognised her, was simply extremely observant or rudely taking a wild guess.

'I apologise,' he murmured, far too cosily for comfort. 'It must be a hard time for you.'

Holly frowned, continuing to act ignorant of his meaning. Twice as composed as she felt and grateful a customer arrived and waited, she said,

'Excuse me,' turning her attention away to acknowledge the woman behind.

In a daze, she took the next order, careful not to alert the suit she was in any way upset or suspicious because of his approach. It was agony waiting out the man seated across the restaurant until he drank his coffee, ate his snack and finally rose to leave.

Aware of his departure, Holly refused to look in his direction in case his presence proved important and she gave herself away by appearing interested. But she followed his progress with quick glances from the corner of her eye. Only when he was outside did she slowly move backward further out of sight into the alcove between restaurant and kitchen to take an emotional breather.

'Did you have an order for me to make up?'

Obsessed with the man outside, Holly jumped at Sid's voice behind her. 'Oh! No.'

'You okay?'

'Not sure.' She glanced out the front restaurant windows. 'Oh my goodness. I don't believe this.'

Sid followed her gaze. 'What?'

'See those two men talking out the front?'

'The suit and the short guy?'

Holly nodded. 'How stupid is that?

They must know in a busy roadhouse that they're on security cameras and being watched. If they're in any way involved or connected to my mother-,' she paused. 'Unless they *want* me to see. Like a threat?'

Sid shook his head. 'Not following, Sunshine.'

The two men looked to be exchanging strong words now. The businessman was pointing a finger at the creep and doing all the talking as though he was in charge.

'They know each other! The little guy checked me out yesterday and, today, Mr. Bearded Office Manager rocks up and claims to know me. Offered his condolences.' Holly gaped at Sid. 'It's not just that little guy out there that's creepy. This is not a coincidence. Mum's body was found, there's publicity and suddenly those two show up. The tall guy looking too much like the man in some of Mum's photographs. Ewan Holt once said that it was always possible the person responsible for Mum's death might return to the area. You keep all the old CCTV footage, don't you?'

Sid nodded. 'Since your mother's disappearance. Police will still have the originals from five years ago and everything since is backed up onto external hard drives and locked in the safe.'

'Right. I'm off to see Gracie.'

Holly strode down the rear passageway and tapped on her office door. Knowing her boss too well to bother with formalities, she opened it and entered.

Gracie peered over the top of her red glasses. 'Looks urgent.'

'Can I call and see if Georgia's free for an evening shift today? I know she's working again tomorrow but if she's free, I can cover the restaurant until she arrives.'

'What you said.' Gracie grinned. 'You seem to have it all worked out. What's happening?'

'Can you spare time to go through the CCTV with me? I need to check the security tape image from five years ago and today with the guy in Mum's photos.'

Gracie frowned. 'Sure but I can phone Georgia while you go get your photos.'

'Damn.' Holly thumped the desk. 'They're still with the police.'

She phoned for Ewan Holt but he was out so she spoke to Sergeant Casey who agreed to send the photos already logged into their computer system and send them to Holly's mobile.

The pings of arrival on her phone soon came while Gracie put in the call to Georgia. After a friendly chat, she hung up.

'The girl's happy to do the shift. Means earning extra money for that trip over the summer.'

'Let's get to it then.'

Sitting in her office chair, Gracie rolled herself across to the live security monitors behind her desk. 'What are we looking for?'

'This man.' Holly brought up the image of the suit on her phone, zooming in with her fingers. 'He arrived less than an hour ago.'

They scanned all the outside live cameras on-screen.

'He just left but might still be out there talking to a short guy,' Holly murmured, standing behind Gracie and peering over her shoulder. 'They might have headed to the carpark. The tall bearded guy was half turned away when he left so his arrival when he walked into the restaurant should have a better face view. Then can we go through the old tapes?'

'Now hold on,' Gracie suggested tactfully. 'The police will have copies of those. Let's find today's images first, okay?'

'Yeah. Of course.'

As Gracie examined all the outside current time videos, she found nothing. When she scrolled back in time and searched, Holly forced herself to drag up a chair and sit down beside her boss, trying to settle her tension. Her mind raced.

Was she being unreasonable, wishing the tall guy to be a match? Was it even remotely possible the man in her mother's photos and the guy outside were the same? At the least, there was a strong resemblance worth checking. He was tall, dark hair smoothly slicked back but with slightly grey streaks now. Similar build and face. Except for the close-shaved beard. A disguise, she wondered?

Holly reined in her impatience and waited for Gracie's results.

'Okay. Found him,' she said eventually. 'Here's the guy arriving. Good front view.' She paused the tape and enlarged it.

Holly held up her phone beside the image on the screen to compare, shocked to see such an eerie similarity.

'Doesn't actually prove anything,' she said, breathless, even a little excited by the possibility there might just be hope yet, 'but it's a solid indicator that someone from Mum's past, possibly with the initials RP, has just boldly approached me. He may not be the killer but he's a connection and therefore of interest, surely?'

Eyes wide, Gracie shook her head. 'You don't need to convince me, honey.

I'd say you're onto a positive worthwhile lead here and the police need to see all this. Since they already have the old security footage, let them put it all together and get busy. They can do video enhancement and all kinds of technical stuff to produce clearer images from car number plates to face photos. Since it looks like the guys have already left, they can track their vehicles.'

Holly paced while Gracie copied today's video footage onto a separate disk. 'I should warn the police that I'm bringing in some more information for them.' She was about to call on her phone but Gracie turned to reach out and place a firm restraining hand on her arm.

'Maybe you should re-think delivering this possible evidence into town by yourself. Remember, we're dealing with a homicide here and those guys might not be at the roadhouse but still lurking around somewhere. How about you phone and mention all this to the Detective or whoever's around. Tell them what you have. Let them come out and collect it themselves. That way you and the tapes are all safe.'

'You think we need to be that careful?'

'Can't hurt. Those guys have shown their hand. If they're in any way connected to your mother's disappearance,' Gracie paused, not elaborating further, 'they won't be playing around. If it turns out to be another false alarm, at least we checked it out.'

'Okay.'

'Don't worry.' Gracie rose and gave Holly a quick hug. 'If the guys are still hanging around somewhere, sitting in a car waiting, and see the police arrive, if they're somehow involved, they might get scared off but they'll be found. We have enough information and video footage to help the police identify and locate them.'

'You're right. The detectives are on it. I should leave it to them.'

'How about when Georgia arrives, she can cover your late shift anyway. The police might want to chat to you and Sid can always use some help in the kitchen so you stay out of sight.'

Holly nodded and phoned the police with her latest findings. 'They'll be out shortly,' she told Gracie as she hung up.

Still restless, she returned to the restaurant until Georgia appeared to take over her shift. When Detective Norton and Sergeant Casey arrived, they questioned Holly and Sophie for a while verifying details about the two men. In Gracie's office, the officers scanned the security video, clearly far more optimistic about this discovery than the last.

Norton never said much but was always quietly observant in the background. Occasionally, he asked a question or made a comment.

Before they left, he murmured casually to Holly, 'Might be wise to keep out of sight until we follow this up. Have company at all times.'

Holly was growing uncomfortable. 'Sure. If you think so. Do these guys know something I don't? Or for some reason believe I do?'

Detective Norton stared her down. 'Do you?' he shrugged.

'You're kidding. What on earth am I supposed to know?'

'Good question. If you can't answer it then we'll see if we can't find those two men. Maybe they can enlighten us.'

'This is all sounding very weird and scary.'

'Stay low,' Norton advised. 'Do you have someone who can be with you?'

Holly exchanged glances with Gracie, her boss' mouth already open to offer. 'You can't. You and the staff are all needed here in the roadhouse. I'll be fine out the front until we close.' She held up a hand as her boss was about to object. 'You're not sleeping in the cabin. You snore. The girls are young and need to get home. I'd feel better if they went back to family and weren't put at risk by being with me. Look, I'll phone Tom. He has to sleep and a strong bloke might be useful.'

Gracie stifled a grin. 'If you say so. I'll let you sort it out. If he can't make it, which I doubt,' she muttered, 'you'll have to wear ear plugs and put up with me.'

'Deal,' Holly agreed feeling her face grow warm with a blush at Gracie's observations.

She stepped out the back into the early evening chill and pressed Tom's number. It rang out for so long she thought her call might go to voicemail but finally he picked up.

Before he could answer, surprised by the influence of his infectious sense of humour, she randomly copied his usual straight-up conversation and jumped right in.

'How would you like to spend the night with me?'

Chapter 8

Taking Tom's previous comment on board about her easy attitude to security, Holly locked her cabin door, forcing him to knock and wait until she answered.

As she opened it, he chuckled, 'You're learning. Now, this invitation was an offer impossible to resist,' he drawled, skimming an arm around her waist so he could pull her close.

'We both need our sleep. Body guard duty only, remember?' she murmured.

'That could mean many things.'

After they thoroughly kissed in greeting, Holly said, 'I'll admit, you're challenging to resist yourself but my head's overloaded to bursting right now. Not sure I would be a worthy partner at the moment.' She paused then whispered, 'I'd rather it be a night to remember.'

'Promise,' he growled, kissing her long and slow again.

When they drew apart and sat together on the sofa, Holly said, 'We've encountered a few new developments in the past twenty-four hours.'

'Don't like the sound of that. What's been happening?'

Holly quietly explained, ending, 'It's only a precaution. It may not become anything but my gut tells me it's likely. The guy was too sure of himself. Had this persuasive arrogance like he was in control and enjoyed it. What I don't understand is why he didn't come forward sooner. Mum's identity has been out there in the news for a week and he only just shows up? If he knew her, I wonder he didn't try to find me previously or contact me after she went missing. I stopped working with the law firm and stayed with friends but I was still in the city. He could have tried to find me if he was so concerned. Or even gone to the police.' Holly shrugged. 'Because it appears he didn't, you have to wonder why not?'

'Maybe back then he didn't see you as a threat. Your mother was still missing. Now she's been found, it's a whole new ball game. The killer, whoever that turns out to be, must know there'll probably be new evidence found, even after all these years. You said the tall guy seemed to be in charge. Maybe he sent in the little guy first to check out the situation up here.'

'That was my thinking, too. If this guy is the RP from Mum's photos and he knew her around the time she disappeared, it doesn't look like the police ever knew or interviewed him back then as an acquaintance.'

Holly frowned. 'I must ask Detective Norton. Unless they did and he had an alibi. Makes no sense him turning up and showing himself, revealing his interest in me, enough to believe he knows I'm Rainey's daughter. You'd think he'd keep a low profile.' She shrugged. 'Maybe he's innocent and just coming forward because of that smug personality.' Holly shivered. 'He's as creepy as the little guy, just in a more stealthy way. To be honest, I'd hate to meet him on a dark night.'

'You won't!'

Judging by Tom's fierce response, Holly was in no doubt she was safe. She only wished there was no need but, for more than one reason, was bolstered to have Tom's presence and support here with her tonight, if only as a precaution.

She longed to show him her gratitude and how much she cared. He had come when she phoned, no questions asked. She would never abuse such loyalty and friendship. Although they were both growing to realise their attraction was swiftly evolving into much more.

Holly couldn't wait to explore a possible relationship with him. When her mother's killer was behind bars. Only then, when the time would be right for her, could she fully open her heart to Tom Searle. For the moment, her nightmare needed to take its natural course and be resolved. The sooner the better.

Until then, out of respect for her mother, her focus must remain on the successful outcome she so desperately wanted. Rainey Duncan's killer. And she would personally make every effort to help make that happen.

Meanwhile, the frustrating uncertainty was taking a toll on her emotions. If it wasn't for the support of everyone in the roadhouse, plus Tom and friends like Billie Gibbs, Holly wasn't sure she would have survived the daily ongoing ordeal this far.

Some days she wanted to disappear into the bush and scream. Others, personally tighten her hands around the neck of whoever stole her mother away forever and squeeze until they choked.

'I've lost you.'

Holly felt Tom's hand gently massaging her back and shoulders. 'Sorry. Wool gathering. Speaking of which, how are the sheep?'

'Hundreds still to go. Shearing's usually weeks. I should leave here as soon as you're safely in the roadhouse in the morning. Get back out to the shed.'

Holly refused to even think that far ahead. She still had Tom's company for the night and planned to appreciate their few precious hours together. 'Sure. Come over to the roadhouse with me in the morning before you go and Sid will make you a hearty breakfast.'

'I'll take you up on that.'

'Least I can do.'

'You don't need to do anything. My pleasure.'

'But for now, we can while away a little time together, right?'

Holly had never known such harmony and contentment with a man before. Maybe because her mother had been so cruelly ripped from her life far too soon and, having never known her father, she feared this wonderful promising relationship with Tom wouldn't last either. With so much else happening at the moment, she could only acknowledge her attraction to the truckie farmer's son and leave it at that.

They enjoyed each other until Holly started yawning.

'I could be offended you find me boring,' he teased.

'Sorry. I have such early morning starts-'

'No need to explain.'

Reluctantly, she rose and showered,

emerging from the bathroom in comfy pyjamas. Tom grinned, not saying a word, as she crawled under the doona.

'My night wear has never been sexy,' she muttered, embarrassed.

'I'm more interested in what's underneath.'

Delightfully shocked by his suggestion, Holly surged with heat and grinned. 'Of course you are and I must admit, I'm flattered. If you play your cards right, it just might be all yours one day.'

Tom's laugh came from deep in his chest. He kicked off his boots, stripped off his windcheater down to a tee shirt and stretched out on top of the covers beside her. When he threw an arm over her, she closed her eyes and smiled.

Later, after she had slept and became vaguely conscious again, Holly heard him prowling the cabin, rattling the door lock before she felt movement beside her and he snuggled up against her back again.

Her morning alarm, always set, buzzed as usual. She groped to shut it off and carefully slid out of bed trying not to disturb Tom. As she dressed, he stirred and rolled over to lie on his back, an arm across his face.

'Morning,' she said. 'A heads up. I leave in five minutes.' He grunted.

'Chirpy first thing, aren't you?'

'Come back to bed,' he drawled.

Holly chuckled. 'Rain check on that one. Get some sleep?'

'Enough.'

While Holly grabbed her phone, tied on her apron and laced up her sneakers, Tom stretched, ambling about the cabin still half asleep, getting fully dressed again. She eyed him looking so adorable. In any other circumstances, she would definitely be persuaded to delay her departure.

When they were both ready for the day, Tom caught her hand and laced their fingers on the chilly walk across to the rear of the roadhouse. Holly unlocked the back door and he held it open.

'Smell that breakfast cooking,' he said, halfway down the passage.

'I know, right? I love arriving first thing. Best start to the day,' Holly agreed.

They greeted Sid as they entered the warm light-filled kitchen.

'How was guard duty?' Sid teased.

'I slept fine. Can't speak for Tom though.'

'Full breakfast for you, mate. On the house.' Sid slid a hot filled plate and cutlery toward Tom. 'Thanks for taking care of our Sunshine.'

Tom acknowledged the comment of

appreciation with a quick nod. 'No problem.'

He settled on a high stool to eat, Holly beside him munching her way through her usual egg and bacon toastie. Tom made short work of his meal and sauntered after Holly into the restaurant.

'Coffee?'

'Sure.'

From his usual order, she knew he liked it strong and black. They stood together sipping hot drinks until Sophie arrived, Gracie did her usual lap around the restaurant and opened up. As on most mornings, early customers, either travelling or needing breakfast on the go, already waited.

Tom poked his head back into the kitchen, thanked Sid for breakfast and kissed Holly, who was deeply aware they were being closely watched.

'Need me tonight?' he murmured.

A loaded offer with double meaning. Holly's body surged with warmth. 'I'll see how today goes and let you know.'

He waved to everyone and headed out.

'Bye, Tom,' Sophie and Gracie chorused loudly together as he disappeared.

'Holly has herself a man,' Sophie said to Gracie, as though she couldn't hear every word.

Taking their teasing in her stride,

Holly shook her head and took her first orders as customers lined up at the counter. She still had today to get through and tomorrow and the day after that. For goodness knows how long. Until it was done.

With her mind still in upheaval mode, Holly did a double take in surprise to see the tall bearded guy come back into the roadhouse again. Understanding she couldn't in any way reveal that she knew he was possibly associated with her mother as he claimed, she took a deep breath. He approached her directly at the counter so she looked him straight in the eye, holding his steely gaze as she served him.

'Good morning, can I take your order?'

'I didn't mean to upset you yesterday.'

Holly paused while she pretended she had just remembered him. 'You didn't. I don't know you.' True enough. 'We get all kinds of people coming through here.' A deliberate slur which provoked the intended reaction.

His eyes glittered and his mouth curled in displeasure. 'I'll just have a coffee. To go,' he growled.

'Of course.' Holly found it difficult to stay serious and not smile at his annoyance.

When he produced a note in payment and handed it over, Holly accepted it and said, 'Cash again. I guess it's safer, right? We can't be too careful these days, risking our personal information being known.'

All said casually enough but when he stared her down, scowling, Holly wondered if she had pushed too far. He was still innocent until proven otherwise. Either way, she didn't care. Prejudiced, she knew. Judging from her firsthand impression at the unfriendly vibes he was sending out, she disliked him, whether he was involved in her mother's disappearance and death or not. Hardly the kind of customer that made your day.

As Holly handed over his coffee, the man murmured, 'Why won't you admit who you are?' The polite businessman image faded, replaced by a rising anger. For whatever reason, he itched for her admission.

She held his hard stare. 'You're a stranger. Who I am is none of your business.'

'What are you afraid of?'

'Not you.' Sounded like a threat. From a man who was troubled by her and what he thought she knew but didn't?

Although in appearance there was a strong resemblance to being her mother's daughter, their dance of words would continue. Holly would never make the admission and acknowledge her identity, least of all to him and certainly never to satisfy his menacing pride. She was not only convinced he was the man in the photos and had known her mother but, because of his seemingly unnatural interest in her, was somehow involved with her disappearance. He was too shrewd by nature not to be but, in fairness, she would reserve her opinion until the police found proof.

And the little guy hanging around was somehow linked, too. Holly was convinced there was some conspiracy between them or they were working together. Because of his probing and interest in her, it was obvious his attention was connected to her mother. Watching Holly, making contact, asking questions, was all too obvious. If they weren't directly involved, they knew who was, so it surprised her they weren't being more careful.

Not experienced criminals or wrongly under the impression they were untouchable perhaps with false alibis for that fateful night five years ago? In their shoes, she would put as much distance as possible between themselves and the location of a violent crime in which they were most likely implicated.

Based on their readiness to listen, questions and following up on any ideas or information, no matter how small or remote in possibility, Holly had complete faith in the police on her mother's case. Detective Norton was a quiet watcher. He would work it all out in the end.

'I'll be watching you,' the man muttered as he left.

Holly wasn't intimidated by his warning. Her only thought was *Why would he need to?* The answer to that question could not be answered soon enough. But it also meant he was not going anywhere and would be sticking around. Concerning, but an advantage if his overconfidence proved his downfall. She could only hope.

The man didn't return that day. The police were informed of his reappearance and intimidation but, at this stage, they could only keep him under surveillance. For now, they kept a low profile, only intending to step in if the man posed a more immediate threat.

By evening, because the guy was probably still around, Gracie nagged and the police agreed, Holly phoned Tom for guard duty again that night.

In her lunch break, frustrated that the man's identity had not yet been confirmed and there was not enough clear

CCTV footage to verify his vehicle and help that process, Holly borrowed Sid's shed key again and rummaged through her boxes for a letter. She knew she had kept it. Like other ideas she had considered so far, it was a slim chance but worth a try.

If she was honest, as much as she had put down roots in a way with Sid and Gracie at the roadhouse, Holly had always only considered it a temporary solution. Never imagining the mystery surrounding her mother would continue unresolved for years. She longed to have her own home one day again where her few belongings, currently stored in boxes, would have their rightful place.

After some searching, the letter she sought was safely found. She tucked the folded paper into her apron pocket, wandered back to the roadhouse and returned Sid's key.

That evening, Sid walked her over to the cabin and stayed until Tom arrived soon after, the deep note of his approaching ute echoing on the still night air.

'I could get used to this bodyguard gig,' Tom greeted Holly warmly.

Eager to share, they settled together on the sofa as usual and she began talking about the idea she thought worthwhile following up.

Holly produced the envelope and unfolded the letter inside, explaining, 'After Mum went missing and I moved up here, I lost contact with most of my friends.' She shrugged. 'I guess it's the price I paid to feel closer to where she was last seen. Mum was pretty much closest to one woman in particular, Susan Rogers, about a similar age. They were nurses working together at the same hospital. Susan wrote to me at our old apartment address in the city after Mum disappeared. She was equally devastated, of course, so I wrote back to her before I moved up here to the Wimmera.

'It's a long shot because it's been years but fingers crossed she's at the same address with the same phone number. Hopefully being evening she might be at home.'

'You're going to call her now?'

Holly nodded. 'Fingers crossed.'

She tapped Susan's old landline numbers into her mobile and waited as it rang out. Suddenly it was snapped up and a familiar voice answered. She gave Tom's a silent thumbs up.

'Susan? It's Holly Duncan.'

She heard the woman's sharp intake of breath. 'Holly. Oh my goodness, I'm so pleased to hear from you. I've been trying to phone your old apartment number and your mobile but, of course, after all this time they're both no longer in use.'

'The police recommended I change it over to a new one after Mum went missing. Just a precaution.'

'Of course.' Holly heard the concern in Susan's voice. 'I so wanted to pass along my condolences.'

She had received only a special few of those so far, except for people who lived and worked close by, and a few regular locals passing through the roadhouse.

'Thank you, Susan. That means a lot.'

'So how are you, dear?'

'It's been a long haul actually.'

'I can imagine. People can't have any idea what you've suffered. I simply can't believe your lovely mother is gone from us all. I miss her dearly and think of you often.'

Holly swallowed against the lump in her throat. She rarely spoke so personally about her mother, nor was she asked, but apart from Susan being an open personality, she had also been her mother's long-time friend, companion and workmate. They had shared so much together and were like sisters.

To avoid breaking down, Holly took herself in hand and inhaled a long deep breath, needing to ease the conversation away from the toughest subject of her life.

'So are you still working at the same hospital?'

'Heavens no, dear. Such a crazy busy environment even back then. After your mother,' she paused, 'I lost heart for quite a time. I resigned, took a break and looked around for something quieter. I'm full time at a local medical clinic these days.'

'Susan, I hope you don't mind but can I ask you some questions about someone I believe Mum knew. I'm hoping you can help.'

'I'll do my best.'

'Since Mum was found recently, I went through some of her old photographs, mainly of her in a group probably before I was born. And then others in which she was with one particular man, probably about the age when she disappeared.'

'Neither your mother nor I were highly social so it would only be one of a few possible people.'

'I know. I don't suppose you have a mobile?'

'Yes I do, dear. Need to keep up with the times,' she chuckled softly.

'Can you tell me the number and I'll send you a few photos.'

'All right. Just a minute and I'll go get it. I've left it in the sitting room beside my chair. Can you hold on a moment?'

'Of course.' Holly only briefly waited before the phone was picked up again. Susan read out the number and Holly noted it down.

'Just putting you on hold Susan while I send you a text and the photos.'

Soon after, on the other end Holly heard the ping of her message arriving on Susan's mobile.

'I have them.'

Holly anxiously waited. Surely if the tall guy RP was a regular part of Rainey's life, as a close and trusted friend, Susan would have known about him. At least, she clung to that hope and quickly tapped her phone onto speaker so Tom could listen in.

'Yes, I definitely recognise him.' Susan's voice had grown distant and small.

Holly's heart leapt, her gaze holding Tom's in anticipation. 'Do you remember his name?'

'Oh, I remember everything about him, dear. Naturally, your mother kept a certain reserve about their relationship and I respected that. He worked in a big city office on Southbank. Something to do with finance I think it was. He was married before but only for a few years. Apparently his wife died young and rather suddenly.'

Another pause from Susan at the other end in which Holly closed her eyes, crossed her fingers and quietly prayed.

'Porter. Robert Porter.'

For a moment, Holly was speechless in relief and shock. In silence, Tom raised his eyebrows and she gave a thumbs up. They had a name and the initials matched. Now the police would have some positive information to work with and investigate.

When she recovered, she said, 'Susan, thank you. Mum had the initials RP on the back of one photo, so it's definitely the same person.'

'There's no trouble is there?' Susan asked warily.

'I haven't told you but I've been living and working in the Wimmera at the roadhouse where Mum was last seen. I just felt-'

'I understand, dear. Go on.'

'Since Mum's discovery and identity were made known by police in the media, Porter showed up here recently. I believed I recognised him. He has a short beard now though which put me off a bit.'

'Be careful, dear. If there was one thing your mother and I disagreed on it was that choice of a friendship. Outwardly, he seemed to be a gentleman and Rainey assured me he was but there was always something about him that bothered me.'

'Can I pass on all this information to the police and tell them you identified Porter? They'll want to speak to you.'

'Of course, dear. As one of your mother's friends, they interviewed me when Rainey went missing. Back then, I mentioned Porter as being a close acquaintance. They would have questioned him, too. Being a smooth operator, I have no doubt he provided a watertight alibi.'

So information on Porter already existed but must be somewhere in her mother's old case files. At least now the police could delve deeper and hopefully connect some dots.

'Having met him now, I know what you mean. Susan, I can't thank you enough but it's getting late. I'll let you know if anything develops from this and promise I'll keep in touch.'

'Please do, dear. I would love to see you again. When you feel the time is right.'

'Absolutely. Bye for now.'

After hanging up, Holly's brain was in such a fog of disbelief and optimism, she felt like she was emerging from another world. But she was clear enough to understand the importance of Susan's verification. She grabbed her holdall and retrieved the card he had given her when they first met to make the call.

'I know it's late but I'm phoning Detective Norton.'

Chapter 9

From his strong tone of voice, Detective Norton latched onto the Robert Porter identity with enthusiasm, complimented Holly on her initiative and promised to follow it up first thing in the morning.

Since Susan Rogers mentioned Porter must have been interviewed when Rainey Duncan disappeared, the police investigation could now connect the content of that initial report to move forward on a deeper background check of his family, business dealings and financial transactions.

Because Porter and the short man were known to each other, Detective Norton was keen to find out how and when the two men met. What threw them together. 'We need to go further back,' he said. 'When we find the link, I believe it will help explain a number of frustrating mysteries in the investigation.'

Excited, Holly hung up. 'So now we wait again.'

'Take it easy until you hear more,' Tom warned softly. 'Not every lead will amount to something.'

'I know. Porter is so mysterious and determined. Yet, if he was interviewed years ago after Mum went missing, he couldn't have raised any red flags or suspicion. Unless they simply couldn't find enough evidence.'

'Proof is the vital key. They'll find it eventually.'

Holly frowned. 'Surely Porter realises that I might mention his persistence and questions to my boss, whether I'm Rainey Duncan's daughter or not? Or even go to the police. Would he risk that potential exposure?'

Tom shrugged. 'He already has. Whatever his reasons, they're strong enough to take the gamble.'

'Well, his lack of caution strikes me as careless. That doesn't fit with the man's personality. The careful way he dresses, the sharp brain that plays mind games. That dogged persistence. It's more than merely a morbid curiosity to pursue the fate of a former romantic interest. When they were together in later years, he would have known Rainey had a daughter. My name. What I looked like. Yet Mum never mentioned him or ever made an effort for me to meet him. It would have been after university when I was working but it still seems odd she kept him a secret. Why?'

'To protect you? Based on what Susan

said, it seems your mother held concerns about him. If she didn't see him as a long term partner, she was probably keeping you at a distance.' He shrugged. 'Need to know basis.'

'And never telling me she was leaving that night. That has always bothered me.'

'Holly, honey,' Tom brushed the back of a hand along her cheek, 'you'll probably never find the answer to that mystery. You need to let it go.'

She leant her head on his shoulder, close to tears. 'I know. I just keep hoping as the police learn more, there might be some logical explanation that comes to light.' After a pause, she said pointedly, 'You don't find it, like, really weird that Susan said Porter's wife died, then Mum was in some kind of relationship with him, *she* disappears, too, and years later her body is found?'

'It could raise questions,' he admitted, 'but Norton and his team will put it all together. It's nearly midnight. You should put on those sexy pyjamas and sleep.'

She tilted her face up to him. 'Never going to live that down, am I?'

He kissed her nose. 'Won't tell a soul.'

She sighed and pulled away from him. 'Has potential for blackmail though, doesn't it? You're going to use it.'

He grinned. 'Thought crossed my mind.'

'Choose wisely,' she whispered, leaning in to kiss him, 'or you may be disappointed.'

'Noted.'

Holly loved Tom's gentle sense of humour. How a glance or a touch stirred her heart. It helped balance out and ease the constant sadness that scarred her life. It could never be a remedy. That would take time as she had long since discovered over the years.

Two years ago, he had casually drifted into the roadhouse and kicked a tiny spark of mutual fascination into life. Both aware but cautious, they had played with it, stalked it, but never chased it down to explore the consequences. What a waste of time, Holly sighed now. All too aware of the fragility and precious nature of existence that could be snatched away in a heartbeat.

Holly and Tom did the usual scooting around each other next morning, getting dressed and ready for their respective days. Breakfast in Sid's kitchen together before Tom disappeared again heading for his father's property and the shearing shed.

Preoccupied with the usual busy morning service, it was mid- morning when her instinct shot to alert. Although the entire roadhouse staff were directed to report his next visit and Holly had prepared herself to expect it at some point, she hadn't anticipated Porter's return so soon.

When she glanced up, he was already pacing the restaurant at a distance. He didn't immediately approach the counter, prowling and watching instead. Once he realised she caught sight of him, he moved forward, aiming directly for her, not Sophie or Alice. Gracie was closely monitoring their CCTV so Holly waited to see if she had noticed and what her next move might be.

For a hot minute, her reaction automatically skipped to defence knowing that while she was in the restaurant, she was protected. But when he flashed that superior smile as though he had the edge in this stalemate situation, her annoyance and impatience snapped. Their guarded exchanges were going nowhere and achieving nothing.

Fed up with his persistence and threats, while also realising she might regret it, Holly decided to deliberately provoke him and see where it led.

She glared. 'Yes?'

'Good to see you again.' His gaze flicked to the embroidered name on her apron. 'Holly.'

'Is it? If you're looking for trouble, you've found it. All staff harassment is reported to police. You might be watching me but you're also being watched now. Mr. Porter.'

That shook him. His attention sharpened at her blunt change in attitude but only for a moment until his mouth curled. 'You're worried.'

'Never.'

'You're her daughter,' he said quietly.

'And how do you know that?'

'Newspapers.'

'What if I am?'

'You admit it,' he pounced, grinning.

'No, I didn't and I'm sure there are many Holly's out there. Why are you so interested in this case anyway? Did you know the victim or are you just a nutter who haunts dead people?'

He stared in silence but because he hesitated and the staff phone buzzed in the alcove behind her, to her annoyance Porter never replied. But it was clear she had him stumped and rattled his confidence.

'Excuse me.'

It was Gracie on the staff line. 'I saw him the moment he arrived. I phoned Norton and he suggested you try and keep him here until he arrives. If you're game, he suggested we try something. When you answer me, speak loud enough that he can overhear.'

Holly immediately raised her voice. 'Not a problem. I can do that.'

'Tell him you finish at midday.'

'Okay.' She pretended to be annoyed. 'I'll clock off at midday and come back for the late shift.'

'Great. He's watching you like a hawk. Hang up now.'

'You're welcome.'

Holly slammed down the phone to maintain her fake mood and returned to the counter. Porter still waited. She hoped he overheard at least some of her side of the conversation. Enough to test if he took the bait.

'You're upset.'

Holly shrugged. 'Change of shift. Order something or move aside.'

Eyeing her steadily, he ordered a full breakfast. With fingers crossed, Holly prayed that meant he intended to stay a while. He paid in cash again, took his table number and moved away.

She personally took his order to Sid in the kitchen. 'This is for our friend. Can you hold it up a bit?'

'Done.'

Later, after a suitable delay, Holly apologised to Alice since she decided to keep her distance from Porter for now and asked her workmate to take over the order and table service.

'He wasn't happy,' Alice muttered on her return.

Holly grinned. 'Made him wait. Want him to hang around until I go off shift for a bit. Hoping he follows me outside. The police are coming and have questions.'

Despite a constant stream of customers, the morning dragged. For a time, Holly thought their plan wouldn't happen. The police didn't appear inside the roadhouse but maybe they were waiting outside in case he left. Porter did disappear for a while but, to her relief, returned ten minutes before her shift change, hovering by the newsstand at the front of the mini market, pretending to browse but flicking regular glances toward the restaurant.

Eventually, just before midday, Gracie appeared from the office behind the counter to supposedly take over Holly's shift. 'Norton has men front and back. You're to leave by the rear and walk straight across to your cabin.'

'They don't have a thing to hold him,' Holly said with despair.

Gracie turned her around and gently directed her away. 'We don't know that. They may learn something. I'm sure it's all under control. Go.'

Reluctant and anxious, Holly did as

she was told, strode down the passageway and left the roadhouse by the back door, placing herself as bait in the path of trouble. Glancing around, she hesitated, surprised and even a little concerned that not a person was in sight. Where were all the policemen Gracie mentioned? Maybe this was what *undercover* meant?

Trusting Norton to keep her safe, whatever they had in mind, she stepped out toward her cabin. Reaching the door and about to unlock it, she heard footsteps crunching on the gravel behind her.

Whirling around, expecting to see a strong man in uniform, Robert Porter leered and gripped her arm instead. 'We need to talk.'

The moment he made physical contact, police bodies emerged from everywhere. Looking both threatening and reassuring, depending on which side you were on, Ewan Holt moved forward, standing eye to eye with Porter who immediately released his hold on Holly.

'Is this man bothering you?'

'It appears so.'

He turned to Porter. 'Are you following this woman, sir?'

'No.'

'Try again. Lost?'

Outwardly ruffled, the operation had clearly shaken him but he recovered and said smoothly, 'Just wanting to pay my respects.'

'Using physical force? I believe you had a little more in mind than that,' Ewan challenged. 'If you would come this way, sir, we'd like to ask you a few questions.' He pointed toward one of the police cars that had cruised up and surrounded them.

'Am I under arrest?'

'Yes.'

'On what grounds?' Porter protested.

'Personal harassment and intimidation.'

'This is ridiculous. I want a lawyer.'

'All in good time. When we get to the station. For the moment, it would be in your best interest to cooperate.'

Fuming at Ewan and flashing one last glare at Holly as he was handcuffed and escorted away, she wondered if Porter would get away with this and continue his bullying. The parallel with her mother's circumstances five years ago was not lost on her. Was this their man or merely a red herring?

Sergeant Casey appeared and checked Holly was okay. Reassured, and before she left with another officer in one of the police vehicles, she said, 'We'll be in touch. Let you know what we find out.'

'Thanks.'

In the restaurant, when Gracie and the girls raised their eyebrows in silent question, Holly shrugged. 'Took him away on a flimsy intimidation charge but not holding my breath they'll get anywhere. He's so sure of himself.'

'Don't be despondent. If Porter's not directly involved, he may lead to whoever is.'

'Nice thought but a slim chance.'

That night, as a precaution, since Detective Norton phoned to reveal the disappointing news that Porter had been released and the police would be in touch tomorrow, Tom came to stay with Holly in her cabin again. By now, they had fallen into an easy routine of familiarity and humour.

'I feel like I'm taking up so much of your time.'

'I'm finished work for the day, Mum's fed me and I have to sleep. If you want the truth, I look forward to coming here every night.'

'And I'm getting used to having you around. You're a good soul, Tom Searle.'

When Detective Norton and Ewan Holt arrived next morning, they all moved into Gracie's office.

'How did it go?' Holly was almost afraid to ask.

'He continued to protest that he was only intending to offer you condolences and, of course, claimed you misunderstood his intentions both in the restaurant and at the cabin. When we queried his interest in your mother, suggesting his regular appearance around the roadhouse looked suspicious, he admitted that he knew her in the past and was shocked at how the situation had turned out.'

'I'll bet,' Holly muttered.

'He refused to answer any further questions until his lawyer arrived. Which meant waiting hours until the guy drove up from Melbourne. I asked why he felt he needed a lawyer for a few simple questions if he had nothing to hide. *It's my legal right,* he said.' Not given to many expressions of emotion, Norton actually managed a slow grin. 'Claimed any publicity would ruin his career and public image. We'll verify his old alibi and dig deeper into every aspect of his life back then and now. He was charged and given a warning. His lawyer will argue the charges in court. Porter will be virtually unaffected. Conduct his business as usual.'

'Maddening,' Holly said.

She knew Norton and his team had Porter's measure. The frustration for everyone this early in the reopened missing person investigation which had become a homicide, lay in lack of proof.

It wasn't always easy but, despite the daily ongoing grind of it all, Holly had to remain positive.

'We did secure a DNA sample from Porter. He refused at first. We can take one without a court order or the person's consent if we have authorization by a senior police officer but only for a hair sample or fingerprints. Once his hotshot lawyer arrived, considering the charges, he could give no reason why the sample shouldn't be taken.' Norton shrugged. 'We're building evidence daily so we'll push on.'

'You have your work cut out, Detective.'

'Sure do, Holly, but we'll get there. We asked Porter about the guy he was with at the roadhouse. Name's Fraser and apparently he's a business associate. Doesn't look like the type of person to be in Porter's social circle. Has a few minor priors so we're checking him out big time.' Norton shook his head. 'The two men just happen to arrive together at the roadhouse in the midst of a homicide investigation where Porter knew the victim?'

'Plenty of coincidence but nothing concrete.'

Norton laid a hand gently on Holly's shoulder. 'Fraser wasn't on our radar five years ago. He is now. The two men are connected. Must mean something. Give us time, Holly. We'll find our man and that's a promise.'

'That's more than I would ever ask.'

'We'll keep in touch.'

The rest of the day was rough. Until she cleaned up in the restaurant, said goodnight to her bosses who both gave her a hug, and headed for the cabin which had become her sanctuary now rather than simply a place to sleep. Because Tom was usually there, his shiny silver ute gleaming in the moonlight and the man himself waiting.

Tonight, she walked straight into his arms and held on tight. Eventually pulling away and being thoroughly kissed.

'Something smells good.' Tom indicated Holly's brown paper takeaway bag.

'Sid sent over some hot chips and a couple of leftover cinnamon donuts.'

'Health food.'

She laughed and they went inside. As they nibbled on the chips while they were still warm and licked their salty fingers, Holly brought him up to date with the day's events.

'Why don't you take your mind off the investigation for a night and all the loose ends still hanging? How about showing me some photos of when you were young? Might help to remember happier times, some positive memories.'

Holly shrugged. 'Heaps of wild red hair even back then. I was just a smaller version of me.'

Tom slowly pulled the ends of the silky scarf she wore when working until the long auburn strands slid free and fell heavily around her shoulders. 'Love to see 'em.'

She retrieved a box and some albums, dragging them across their knees as they sat on the sofa. Holly began opening packs of old colour prints she hadn't seen in years.

'You were gorgeous even as a kid.'

'I was kind of cute, wasn't I?'

'Modest, too.'

'When I complained about my hair, Mum would sit me down and brush it until it shone then make me look in a mirror. She would spread it out around my shoulders and make me admit that it was beautiful hair and nothing less. Adamant that I should never cut it short. She was always so positive and, now that I think about it, always happy really. Said I was all she needed.'

'I would have loved to meet her,' Tom murmured.

'Lordy, she'll be looking down and loving you back. You're a good and handsome bloke, Tom Searle, and no mistake. She used to tease me for not going out much on dates and stuff. Said I was too serious. Any time a handsome man showed some interest and I was in doubt, she always said, *You'll never find out if he's the right one until you get to know him.*'

'Wise words.'

Holly pulled a face. 'Obviously none of them worked out in the past. And since I've been living here, I haven't made the time or felt any interest in guys and dating. Until you walked into the restaurant.'

'From the first time I set eyes on you and we didn't say much, I felt like I was loving a stranger. Now I feel like I've known you all my life.' He kissed her slow and gentle. 'I'd only be half alive without you.'

'I feel the same,' she whispered, 'but you're learning more about me and I hardly know much about you at all.'

'That's for another time. Tonight you need to find a happy place. You said you don't have many keepsakes from your mother. Except that old clock up there.'

He nodded toward the mantel where, as always, it sat unwound and silent on its shelf. 'Want me to wind it up?'

'Guess I should. Mum loved that old thing and always kept it running. *Don't forget to keep grandma's clock wound up,* she would say. *Take care of it. Don't lose the key. Make sure you always keep it in the drawer at the back.* Lost count of the time she told me that.'

'Does it even go?'

'Not since Mum went missing,' Holly admitted softly. 'I guess so. I feel bad for not attaching more importance to it.'

'How about we give it a try?'

Holly grinned. 'Sure.'

Tom rose and carefully carried the clock to Holly's small table and opened the drawer at the back. He held up the winding key then frowned.

'Looks like your mother even left you a reminder note,' he said, as he handed a tiny bundle of folded paper to Holly.

'Pardon?' As she accepted it and pressed it with her fingers, she shook her head. 'No, it's hard inside. Something's wrapped.'

As Holly unfolded the tiny scrap of paper, a small flat key fell onto her lap. 'Another one?' She flattened out the crumpled paper. 'It's Mum's handwriting.' Out loud, she read, '*I fear my life is in danger. Use this information wisely.*' Horrified at this revelation, Holly glanced at Tom. 'Underneath there's the name and address of a city bank and a safety deposit box number.'

Shocked and mystified, they stared at each other.

Chapter 10

Holly placed a hand on her chest, her heart thumping, her mind reeling from her mother's fateful words. 'We need to let Detective Norton in on this. I have to go to Melbourne.' Still distracted, she frowned, *'Use this information wisely?* Tom, this could be the key to everything. She knew she was in danger.'

Her heart and mind crumpled as she was struck by the heartbreaking reality of their tragic discovery. Yes, it was a stunning and promising find but Holly knew it would take her a long time to process not unearthing it sooner.

'You know what this means?' she groaned. 'If only I'd wound up that damn clock and looked in the back drawer, I would have found this five years ago. It might have helped solve Mum's disappearance and saved so much pain.'

'Don't get ahead of yourself. We don't know what your mother locked in that box.'

'I've wasted five years' worth of days.' Feeling helpless and inadequate, she threw her arms into the air. 'All the tears. The nightmares. Damn it!'

Tom drew her into his arms and held her tight. 'Stop beating yourself up. It won't change anything. We have the note and key now. Resolution starts here.'

After a while, Holly pulled back and swiped at her tears. 'Yes, it does, doesn't it? Mum sent me a message. At least it's been found. Sorry I kind of went off the rails there.'

He kissed her softly. 'Never apologise for having emotions. This key might give us enough information to find the answers. Even some evidence to back it up. But you need to tread carefully here and not go alone. You need company or police backup.'

'I can't go until morning anyway but if I leave really early, I can be down there when the bank opens.'

'It's a four hour drive. You plan on getting up and heading off at five?' Tom didn't wait for her answer and his voice was firm. 'You're not going alone.'

Holly closed her eyes for a moment and reopened them, grinning. 'And if I don't?'

'No more sleepovers,' he growled, trying to look serious and failing.

Holly chuckled. 'I'm taking that key to bed with me.'

'Ouch. Three's a crowd.'

She rolled her eyes. 'But unless I

have a nightcap, I won't sleep.'

By the time she changed, Tom had poured them each a brandy. When Holly emerged from the bathroom, he said, 'Just googled and found out you'll need identification with that key for a safety deposit box.'

'My driver's licence?'

Sitting cross legged on the bed, drinking together, they set their phone alarms for five. Conversation was low and fitful and unimportant, both with their minds on the following day and what it might reveal.

After a while, she murmured, 'So I'm guessing you want to tag along?' Tom grinned and raised his eyebrows but stayed silent. 'How's that going to work with shearing?'

'I'll text Dad and he can arrange another worker for the day.'

'Have it all worked out, don't you?'

'Thanks for asking. Whether it's me or someone else going with you, it eases my mind.'

'I wouldn't choose anyone else but it's rather sweet to see you all manly and protective,' she teased. 'Sid will already be in the kitchen when we leave. I'll drop in and maybe grab some breakfast for us both. But I'll need to text Gracie so she can organise my replacement. Probably Georgia. It's almost end of term and spring holidays are coming up. She'll welcome the work.'

It was still dark when Holly and Tom jostled around each other, half awake and neither really having slept properly. When they were dressed and ready to step out the door, Holly sent off a text to Detective Norton with all the details of their key find, the address of the bank in Melbourne and their trip plan. She also promised to give him progress reports of their location along the way and to keep an eye out for any closely following vehicle.

Before they left the cabin, Tom stayed a hand on her arm and said, 'How about you slink low behind me, jump into my ute from the driver's side and keep your head down. Give me your roadhouse key and I'll nip into Sid to give him a heads up and grab breakfast. That way, anyone watching will think it's just me leaving and you're still inside.'

'You reckon Porter is still around and would go that far?'

He shrugged. 'Let's take every precaution until Norton's done his full background on the man and we hear what he has to say.'

Crouching behind Tom, Holly had to stop herself from breaking into a giggle. He unlocked his ute, opened the door wide and stepped back, pretending to check his phone while Holly snuck in front of him, keeping low.

In five minutes he returned with their bagged restaurant breakfast from Sid, didn't say a word and backed up. He only flicked on the headlights when he was halfway along the drive like he always did so as not to disturb the occupants of other cabins who would still be sleeping.

Keeping to his usual routine in case anyone had ever watched him and wouldn't see any suspicious change, he turned and drove around to the front of the roadhouse and out onto the highway. The direction he always headed for a few miles until he turned off down the gravel road past his farm and further out to his father's property where he had been wool classing all week.

But not today.

'Stay low,' he murmured once they sped up, constantly checking for headlights close behind in his rear mirror. 'Okay, all good. Let's eat. Those hot toasted sandwiches smell good.'

Traffic was light out in the country at this hour of the morning with only transports and an occasional other vehicle on the road.

By daybreak an hour along, Holly said, 'I could go a coffee.'

She noticed Tom checked all his

mirrors and only pulled into a takeaway drive-through when he was satisfied. That way neither of them had to leave the vehicle although later, after much watching and double-checking, Tom made a roadside bathroom stop in a small highway town. With his usual warnings to *make it quick* and *keep low*.

Within two hours, they had left the two lane country roads behind and joined the freeway, the capital city getting closer with every kilometre.

'We're making good time,' Holly checked her phone clock. 'Allowing for morning commuters and getting through the suburbs, we should make it soon after bank opening.'

'I've been keeping an eye on vehicles behind us and passing.'

'I noticed.'

'They're all turning off. No long-term followers. Fingers crossed we don't have a tail.'

After three hours, around eight, Holly's mobile rang. 'It's Detective Norton,' she said and put it on speaker. 'Morning. We're about an hour out. I can send you my road map location.'

She heard the humour in Norton's voice. 'Been tracking you since you left.'

'Oh. Of course.'

'Also tracking Porter's number, too.

He's near the roadhouse.'

Holly and Tom exchanged a glance. Interesting. 'He's still around and believes I'm at work?'

'Apparently. Don't have eyes on him but he's either parked or camping out. We'll have an unmarked vehicle follow you once you reach the city. I'll text you the registration and there'll be a plain clothes waiting at the bank.'

'How will we recognise him?'

'We'll only assign an officer at the last minute and text you his identification when you arrive. That will include a photo, badge number and so on.'

'Thanks.'

'Safe driving.'

Holly hung up and sighed. 'It all sounds so undercover. If Porter's still back in the Wimmera, I wonder if it's all necessary.'

'No harm in taking precautions. Police have our back and we'll stay sharp.'

'Speak for yourself. I'm usually on my feet all day. Can't wait to get out of this ute.'

An hour later, Holly was well and truly over it as they crawled from one red light to another. 'I've rarely returned to the city since Mum's disappearance,' she said in reflection.

'Forgot how busy and noisy it can be.'

Eventually they reached the underground carpark for the bank building in the CBD. Holly yawned and stretched as she stepped from the ute.

'I'm starting to get an idea of what your long haul road trips might be like.'

Tom chuckled as she checked the deposit box key and her driver's licence were safely tucked into an inside zipper pocket of her carryall. She slung it over her shoulder and they walked to the lift.

Riding up just the one level to ground floor reception, Holly took a deep breath as the lift doors slid open and they stepped out. As promised, only minutes before Detective Norton had sent a photo and details of the officer to watch out for and she recognised him immediately. Apart from the slightest nod, the man made no other move or indication they had arrived.

'Are we supposed to ignore him?' Holly said.

'Guess so. He knows we're here and will tell Norton.'

'Will he follow?'

'We'll soon find out,' Tom grinned. 'Relax. Let's do business.'

Once they announced the purpose of their visit and a female bank employee was appointed to assist them, looking smartly outfitted and extremely official in a navy suit, they followed her as she escorted them toward the back of the main floor.

With the attendant's digital pass, they went through two sets of security doors before entering a large square room with rows of numbered security deposit boxes. Having already shown her identification, the young woman located their number, smiled and inserted her key into one of the locks.

'Your key now,' she said, 'then we turn them together.'

With her hand shaking for no reason other than anticipation for what the box might contain, Holly inserted and turned her key in unison and the lock clicked open.

'There are cubicles for your privacy,' the attendant indicated small rooms to one side, 'and I'll come back when you're done. Just use the buzzer by the door.'

'Thank you.' Holly slid out the metal box. 'It's not heavy,' she said to Tom once they were inside one of the cubicles. 'I'm almost afraid to open it.'

After a second's hesitation and tension building in her stomach, she lifted the hinged lid. The only contents were a square sealed box marked DO NOT OPEN and two large envelopes, obviously both containing some kind of paperwork.

While Tom stood aside, she said, 'One is labelled to be opened first.'

She took up a seat beside Tom and unsealed the first one containing photographs, and pages of typed notes addressed to Holly.

They flicked through the photographs of Robert Porter alone or Porter and her mother dressed up at various functions. All dated and labelled on the back. There was also a folded newspaper article about a house fire and the body of woman found in the blaze. As yet unidentified but the female resident was missing. Without a name, it didn't make sense.

'Mum must have included this for a reason.'

Holly turned to the typewritten pages and hesitated, finding it difficult to face the words her mother had put down in what would have been a desperate situation at the time.

'It's dated a week before she went missing.'

'*My darling Holly,*' she began reading softly aloud, '*if you are reading this, I have failed. Please forgive me. This information pertains to a man named Robert Porter who I met and dated briefly when I was young. Before I met your father.*'

Shocked by that declaration, Holly stopped reading for a moment.

'Porter had been married before,' she continued, 'but only for a few years as his wife, Linda, died suddenly in a fire at their house.'

'That's what the newspaper cutting is about,' she murmured.

'I learned later that they were separated and in the middle of divorce proceedings.

'In the beginning, I felt sorry for Robert as he played on my sympathy over his wife's death. He was a considerate gentleman, quite dashing and swept me off my feet for a while attending dinners and formal functions, all connected with his business life. He made me aware I should feel privileged to be attending with him. I soon discovered the attention was a façade when he became jealous and overbearing.

Later I found out the house fire that caused Linda Porter's death appeared to be under suspicious circumstances but no strong evidence was ever found nor any conviction ever made. In these instances, the husband is often the main suspect, and Robert was no exception considering the bitter legal battle in his life at the time.

He tried to convince me that the media reports and police interviews were wrong. He had an alibi at the time his wife died, claiming to be in Sydney on *business. I always thought it a disturbing coincidence that she died prior to the divorce when Robert stood to benefit both from house insurance from the fire and life insurance on Linda's death. From his hints, I gather it amounted to over a million dollars. I was sceptical when he claimed Linda was only divorcing him for his money and that she "got what she deserved". I was horrified at those words.*

I tried to end my relationship with Porter but he was persistent and wouldn't give up. But because of his controlling nature, I no longer had any interest or respect for him. He was angry and took the break badly.

As a coincidence about the same time, I met your father. I was at a dance in a group with Susan Rogers and other nursing friends and their partners, mainly medical people. Only one man was a lawyer and I was immediately drawn to him.'

Holly paused and gasped. 'My father was a lawyer?' It seemed her interest in the law was no coincidence. Tom squeezed her hand and grinned.

Continuing, she read, *'At first sight, I was already half in love with your father and soon fell all the way. Porter tried to disrupt and interfere with my new relationship in an effort to* win me back I suppose. But there was never any chance he would succeed.

Sadly, your father, the love of my life, was only briefly in it. We were deeply in love and planned to marry. I had only just discovered I was pregnant with you and we were so excited for our future but your father met with a road accident and was killed.'

Holly raised a shaking hand to her mouth and tears welled in her eyes.

'To my eternal regret, I never told you all this and I should. But it was the deepest pain of my life and you were my richest blessing from that brief lovely time. You deserved to know, of course, and asked me many times but I simply could not face the explanation. I always suspected interference with your father's vehicle but nothing was ever proven.

Before you were born, Porter continually called and visited me. Your grandma was a tigress and kept him at bay, saying I was grieving and he should have more respect. In the hospital after you arrived, Porter brought flowers, saying he would care for us both. I was disturbed at the thought. I told him the truth. I loved your father and would never love another.

While we lived with Grandma Duncan for a few years Porter was trouble and *still pushing into my life. I knew we needed to move away which was when we lived in the country for a time and you started primary school. I was as careful as possible, keeping our identity and lives as quiet as possible. After grandma became ill, I was forced to return to the city with you to care for her until she died.*

To keep a low profile, we had a private funeral and I sold the house quietly and privately. Or so I thought. Porter tracked us down and forced his way back into my life again. He stalked grandma's house waiting for me to appear. He approached me and tried to restart our friendship. I was terrified, especially when he mentioned my beautiful daughter and I worried that, now he had found us, you would also be in danger.

We moved into our apartment, changed our phone numbers, changed jobs and made sure both of us were with other people as much as possible. Certainly never alone at night. Porter was occasionally in the social pages of newspapers with other women and I prayed he had moved on. I was mistaken.

He reappeared, haunting me, making threatening suggestions about you. I suspected I would never be rid of him unless I took action of some kind. This is why I am now writing details to you. I had researched Linda Porter's death and your father's death, as far as I was able in old newspaper archives and public records. So much mystery, never resolved. I hope one day it may be so.

In recent weeks, to gain Porter's confidence, I have pretended the possibility of rekindling my friendship with him. I suggested time alone together to talk. Get reacquainted. I have rented a cottage in the country and my plan is to meet him there, get him talking and record any possible admission or comments that might implicate him. I am trusting his arrogance may cause him to boast. To my shame, I am even prepared to sleep with him to achieve it.'

Holly glanced at Tom. 'Then she's just signed her name. She took a risk and it claimed her life. If only she had gone to the police with her concerns instead. She was heading up to the Wimmera to meet Porter and get some kind of confession. I'm surprised she even considered it knowing him as she did. He had no intention of meeting her. He made sure he had an alibi and was far away that night. So who followed and killed her? It had to be someone who knew where Mum would be that night. And that was Porter.'

'This evidence is significant,' Tom

162

said, shaking his head. 'It's basically a signed statement. More important than the key that unlocked the box where it's been for years. You'll hand it over to the police officer outside for safekeeping?'

'Why?'

'More than one suspicious death has happened around Porter. What if he saw through your mother's attempts to renew their friendship and lure him away? What if he suspected or discovered she had written evidence that implicated him? That could be why he's hanging around you at the roadhouse. You're the most likely person to possess it.'

'Who else would have known Mum wrote such information and passed the knowledge on to Porter? She was such a private person and would never have trusted anyone with such valuable information.'

'Can't answer that one.'

'One of too many crucial unanswered questions.' Holly frowned. 'Based on this letter, Mum would never have trusted anyone. I'm not handing over the second envelope. That's personal. I know it.'

Holly grabbed her mobile, turned on its camera and began snapping each photograph front and back, and every page her mother had written from the first opened envelope.

'Now we have a copy. I'll send all the images to your phone and to Detective Norton as well. The original is most important. We need to get it to him as soon as we get home.' Holly stowed the contents back into the envelope.

'Are we good to go?'

Holly nodded, slid the empty security box back into its slot and buzzed for the attendant who returned and escorted them from the vault.

'We've covered our bases. Nothing more we can do until we get back to the Wimmera and see what the detectives make of Mum's information about Porter's true personality and harassment.'

The police officer was still standing where they left him. Being inside the bank with their video surveillance plus no doubt radio contact with Norton at all times. He would have been alerted if any problems arose.

As they passed, they acknowledged him with a nod which was returned.

'Want to grab some lunch?' Tom asked in the lift back down to the basement.

Holly hesitated. 'Much as I'd love a glass of wine and long lazy lunch with you, maybe another time? We should probably grab something to go, rather than be out in public. Especially since we're in possession of this lot.' She tapped her bulging carryall and its additional contents.

'Sure. We'll find a drive-through. I wonder what's in the box you're not to open?'

'Probably be an explanation in the second letter.'

'Are you going to open it soon?'

'Not yet. Mum clearly labelled the first envelope for a reason.' She paused. 'I believe I know what's in the second one. It's about my father.' Tears pooled in her eyes. 'Just from Mum to me. I'll read it alone when we get home.'

'Sure.' Tom slid an arm around her shoulder and drew her close.

'Have you followed my instructions exactly?'

'Of course.'

'You kept out of sight?'

'Yeah.' Annoyed.

'I see they're leaving the bank in his ute. Don't lose them.'

'Clever that. Tapping her phone.'

'You get the piece?'

'Of course.'

'We need the goods.'

'Yeah, yeah.'

'I mean it. Don't fuck up like last time.'

'I know what I'm doing. And you ain't gettin' the goods until I'm paid.'

'We'll meet as arranged after it's

done.'

    'This is the last job. I ain't doing any more.'

    'We'll discuss that later.'

    'I mean it. No more. You promised.'

Before they left the underground car park, Tom said, 'Mind if we hide the envelopes and box in a storage area behind the back seat?'

Holly shrugged. 'If you think we need to, sure. I guess it doesn't hurt to take extra precautions.'

Once through the city and suburbs, Tom pulled into a drive-through takeaway and they stopped in the carpark only long enough to eat then continue.

More than halfway home, having left the freeway and now cruising on the two lane country road, Tom muttered, 'I reckon we might have a tail.'

Weary, Holly had her eyes shut almost dozing but sat up and leaned around to see who was following.

'He's been there a while. Can you get a photo?'

'He's not close but I'll try.'

She whipped out her phone, zoomed in and clicked a few times, sending the images off to Detective Norton with a short text of explanation about their situation. He would know their location.

'How did someone find us if Norton says Porter's still in the Wimmera?'

'With the right app, anyone can track and tap phones these days,' Tom said.

A short time later, Holly's phoned buzzed. 'Rego's not clear enough to identify. 'They're sending the highway patrol to intercept and check it out.'

Tom frowned. 'How far away?'

'Didn't say.'

They stayed vigilant, Tom constantly checking his side and rear view mirrors. 'Tail's edging closer. Looking more suspicious by the minute.'

'No sign of the patrol car yet.'

As they drove a long quiet stretch of straight road with light traffic in both directions, the trailing vehicle made its move. As soon as they saw a sign for a passing lane ahead and reached it, their tail closed up behind them and began to overtake.

'We're in for some action.' Tom looked straight ahead, concentrating on driving. 'When he's level, as he passes, see if you can't get a photo.'

With the four wheel drive alongside them, Holly raised her phone again, zoomed in and clicked. 'You know what? I think it's that short creepy guy from the roadhouse. Think Norton said his name was Fraser.'

'No kidding,' Tom growled. 'Bastard.'

Not only did the vehicle stay level with them but it slowly edged closer, threatening.

'He's trying to force us off the road. Hang on.'

Holly grabbed for the hand rail above the window. Gripping the wheel tight, Tom slowed and edged the ute further left with two wheels in the gravel but keeping two on the safety of the sealed road. Matching their speed, the other car still drove side by side then suddenly veered close and slammed against them.

Their ute swerved but Tom held his line and, when the passing lane ended, prayed for an oncoming vehicle, forcing the guy to retreat. But their adversary swung away then back toward them and thumped then again. This time, all four wheels of the ute slid off the bitumen and into loose roadside gravel. As Tom grappled to steady the ute and keep a straight line, Fraser sped up and cut them off, forcing Tom to jam on the brakes, heading over rough grassy ground toward a fenced paddock. Holly hung on tight and held her breath as the front bumper stopped just short of the fence, giving it a nudge.

With lightning speed that surprised them both, considering his height and size, Fraser was out of the other vehicle and dashing toward them, a handgun aimed directly at Tom in the driver's seat.

'Stay there,' Tom warned in a low voice. 'He wants that information, not us.'

'He's not getting it,' Holly said fiercely.

'Damn right he's not.'

Fraser waved the gun and yelled, 'Get out.'

Tom slowly undid his seat belt, opened his door and stepped out. He towered over Fraser. If a gun wasn't pointed at him, Holly was convinced Tom would easily take him down.

'And the girl,' Fraser bellowed.

Deliberately slow, Holly eased from the passenger side and walked around the back of the vehicle.

'Stop right there. Hand over the information.'

Straight-faced, she spread her arms wide. 'We don't have it.'

'I'm not stupid. Do it.'

'We handed it to the police. We're being tracked. Now we're stopped, the police will come check. You don't have much time.'

Fraser stepped closer. 'Then go get the stuff.'

'I just told you, I can't.' She gestured toward Tom's vehicle. 'Go look for yourself.'

'Where is it then?'

'Safely in the hands of the police. We gave it to an officer while we were in the bank.'

At that announcement, Fraser's face contorted and he began to look rattled. He waved his gun toward the fence. 'Both of you, over there.' He produced a pair of handcuffs and handed it to Tom. 'Tie yourselves together.'

When they did as he asked, Fraser growled, 'Don't move,' and strode over to the vehicle. He dragged Holly's large carryall from the front and upended it so all the contents fell onto the ground. Then he appeared to be scrambling around in the glove box, searching under the front seats before moving to the back.

'What if he finds it?' Holly whispered.

'Doubt it.'

'I haven't read Mum's other letter. And the box.'

Tom shook his head. 'Be okay. Stay calm. What you said shook him. Smart.' He grinned.

They watched as Fraser frantically rummaged in the back, looked under and around the seats but didn't bother to drop them down and search behind. He turned his attention to the ute tray. It had a tarp cover which he unbuttoned, flung back and thoroughly searched. Then he lay on the ground and checked under the vehicle.

'Where the hell is that patrol car?' Holly said.

It had probably only been about ten minutes since they made contact with the police but with everything that had happened, it felt much longer.

'Might not have been close.'

'Hope they only use sirens. Might scare him off before they get here.'

Coming up empty handed and hearing them talk, Fraser strode back toward them again. 'What are you talking about?'

'Just saying, you're wasting your time. We don't have it.'

'You're lying. And there's no police coming either.'

Holly wondered if it would do any good to get him talking and distracted. 'I recognise you from the roadhouse.'

'So what?'

'Porter your boss?'

Tom shook his head and frowned a glance of caution but Holly was in the mood for stirring things up.

'You know you can't trust him.'

'Shut up.'

'Bet he's let you down.'

Fraser flashed her a glare that seemed to have touched a nerve. He produced a phone, moving a distance away with his back turned but in the stillness of the bush, Holly caught snatches of his murmured conversation.

'It ain't here … I searched … I'm out.'

Without even glancing in the direction of his hostages, Fraser strode for his vehicle.

'They'll catch you,' Holly yelled after him.

He jumped in his vehicle and revved it backward. He screeched out onto the road, turned and sped back the way he came.

'Want to bet he phoned Porter?'

Holly nodded. 'I hope they panic and make mistakes.'

'Just damn glad Fraser didn't put a knife through my seats.'

Handcuffed together, Holly grinned. 'Could be worse.'

Tom chuckled and bent to kiss her. Moments later, as he and Holly kept each other warm by snuggling close, the classy blue and white checked patrol car finally arrived, its lights flashing. The two officers emerged and while one checked them out making sure they were okay, the other one unlocked the cuffs.

Tom pointed south the way they had come. 'It was Fraser. Didn't find what he came for. My ute's damaged but okay. Go get him. We'll be fine.'

The officers radioed the situation back to Norton, jumped back in their vehicle and, within moments, lights and sirens blaring, took off in pursuit.

'Don't like Fraser's chances.' Holly shivered.

Tom drew her into a warm hug for a moment. 'Let's get back into the ute and turn on the heater. You okay?' She nodded. 'Wouldn't hurt to talk this out with someone. Maybe tomorrow?'

'I feel limp. I was more worried about losing that second letter and the box than having a gun pointed at us. Glad you're driving.'

Detective Norton phoned. 'Tom's car is battered on the driver's side,' Holly said then assured him they were okay and safely on the road again heading home.

'The highway patrol will have Fraser in custody soon. See what we can learn.'

Almost home, when her body and mind had settled more, Holly said, 'That was the best idea about hiding the stuff.'

'Fraser thought stealing it would be a walkover. To be honest, he didn't seem all that committed to searching the ute too deep. I'd say he's been doing Porter's dirty work for years.'

'Yeah. That man might have a smooth mouth but he's a coward.'

'A predator disguised as a friend.'

The driver talked on his mobile while he sped. 'They didn't have the stuff.'

'Did you search properly?'

'Course. Girl claimed they handed it to a cop in the bank.'

The other man swore. 'You believed her? She was lying, you idiot. Get rid of the gun?'

'Course. If I get caught, you make bail or I talk.'

'Just a glitch. Don't be hasty. We'll get it.'

'No. I'm done.'

The line went dead.

As Holly and Tom pulled into the roadhouse, police vehicles were parked out front, the officers apparently waiting inside. Tom retrieved the envelopes and box from under the back seat. Holly took charge of the second envelope and box, sliding it into her carryall for later.

Her composure crumbled when she saw Gracie step forward and pull her into a hug. 'You're home and safe now.' Words that touched Holly's heart and brought tears.

Georgia and Reilly hung around nearby. 'Sophie said to say hi and she'll see you in the morning.'

'Thanks for covering for me.'

Detective Norton, Ewan Holt and Louise Casey hovered in the background.

'They want to talk,' Gracie said.

'You need to freshen up first?'

Holly shook her head. 'I'd love a strong coffee.'

'Done.' She beckoned to Georgia. 'You heard the woman. Bring a round for everyone into my office.'

Once Holly and Tom were seated, the officers standing, she handed over the original of her mother's letter of information to Detective Norton.

He laid a hand gently on Holly's shoulder. 'A great find that gives our investigation a boost. Throws a whole new light on a number of cases. Your mother hid it well.'

Holly nodded, understanding. It was a bittersweet discovery but as a result of finding and reading the first letter, pieces of her life's puzzle were slowly beginning to fit together and make sense. She vaguely recalled that her mother had said she dated a handsome businessman who made her feel special. When Holly had asked what happened, Rainey had simply replied that it didn't work out. She chose not to keep in touch and he was no longer a part of her life. Even though her mother had written it in the letter, Holly had forgotten they briefly spoke about it many years earlier.

And on that fateful day her mother left, not knowing it would be for the last time, she had been hugged extra tight and sent safely to stay with friends.

Holly's energy level dropped, her body felt heavy, overwhelmed with emotions both high and low in recent weeks and after today's long drive and drama. Her mother's body being found; knowing the deepest burden until her mystery disappearance was fully solved, then grief on confirming her death; the restrained excitement of getting to know Tom; disappointments in seeking answers for the crime and, most alarming today, being held up at gunpoint in the bush. Holly let out a ragged sigh.

'You all right, Holly?' Gracie asked softly as Georgia brought them all hot drinks, handing them around.

She nodded. 'Looking forward to sleep.'

'Not without the pair of you eating something first. When we're done here, Sid will make you something light.'

'I'll make it quick, Holly,' Norton said. 'We'll delve into Linda Porter's death again and both of your parents' deaths. Your mother didn't mention your father's name?'

'She wrote another personal letter to me. I haven't opened it yet. I'll let you know as soon as I read it.'

Norton nodded. 'Appreciate it. Tom, you and Holly need to come into the station to make your statements. In the morning?'

Tom and Holly shared a glance and nodded.

'All three events appear to be connected and suspicious.' His phone beeped and he checked it. 'Fraser's been caught and arrested. They're bringing him to the police station now so I'll head back into town shortly. He'll be charged with common assault and false imprisonment, both serious offences with potential prison terms. He'll stay in custody overnight to appear in court tomorrow morning. In the circumstances, with your statements, he may plead guilty and the court will decide what punishment. If he doesn't, it will go to trial. He may be offered bail but can't leave the country. If not, he'll be held on remand until the hearing.

'We've already established that Fraser's on record for minor offences but no major crime. His movements and alibis for the three lives under renewed investigation will be checked. Same for Porter but he seems to keep his distance so we still have to dig into his movements and the belly of that connection between the pair of them for the dates in question. We'll check bank records. See if any withdrawals and deposits match between Porter and Fraser at similar times. Check on possible money trails.

'So you know,' he addressed Holly personally, 'a person can be charged with *conspiracy to murder* if they arrange for someone else to do the job, or even simply encourage or persuade someone to murder another person. If Porter has a hold over Fraser, we'll learn about it.'

'Good to know,' she murmured. 'Hope it means a long term in prison.'

'Maximum penalty's up to 14 years but we need more proof. We'll find it. We have a lot more new information now and every spare man on the job. There'll be clues buried deep somewhere that will crack every single one of those three cases. Count on it.' Norton shuffled, head down. 'We lost track of Porter after the highway incident. Must have ditched his phone. Probably bought another one by now. So he's temporarily off our radar. He may be watching you and Tom.'

He glanced at Gracie, who shook her head. 'Hasn't been to the roadhouse. Nothing on CCTV.'

Norton paced. 'Giving us the slip suggests he's worried and hiding. Getting desperate.'

Aware of the day's trauma for Holly and Tom, Norton ended their session. As always, promising to keep in touch with even the smallest development. And because Porter was missing, they all knew to remain vigilant.

After the police left, although Holly was exhausted, she was determined to read her mother's letter. First, Gracie made her eat. In Sid's kitchen, with Tom sitting close, Holly briefly recapped the gist of her mother's first letter statement as Gracie and Sid listened in amazement.

'Damn glad you found it, Sunshine,' Sid murmured.

'It was Tom's idea. I just had grandma's old clock sitting there idle. After all the years Mum nagged me to keep it wound and running. He suggested I get it going again.'

Gracie glared at Holly. 'You're not staying alone tonight.'

'I need to read Mum's letter. I'll be fine.'

'No, you won't. Lock your cabin door, don't open it to anyone and let me know when you're ready. I'll come over and stay the night.'

Barely able to keep her eyes open, Holly was too tired to argue. Tom walked her to the cabin, lingered at the door and said goodnight.

'I'll call,' she whispered between kisses.

Holly reluctantly watched him leave, cringing at the sight of his damaged vehicle as he drove away, went inside and locked the door. She removed the box from her carryall and set it on her bedside table, then her mother's second letter, almost afraid to start reading. Taking a deep breath, she opened the envelope, withdrawing typed pages and another separate sealed envelope which surprised her. Instinct told her to deal with the letter first.

'Darling, Holly, I will be forever regretful and hope, in time, you can forgive me but desperation has finally forced me to tell you about your father. In the sealed envelope is a DNA report confirming his identity and paternity, and also his birth and death certificates.'

Holly took a moment to process that declaration and knew she was about to learn much more.

'Your father was John Anderson Mitchell.' So she was *Holly Elizabeth Duncan-Mitchell!* *'You will see from his birth certificate where he was born and his parents. As I write this, your Mitchell grandparents are both still alive.'*

The words blew her away. Being an only child, this was a stunning revelation. Her mother had also been an only unexpected child of her Duncan grandparents who had married late but were now both gone. Holly was excited to finally discover the truth about her father's family.

'Your Mitchell grandparents, Paul and Carol, live near Daylesford on their farm in a small bungalow. John was their oldest son and a lawyer as you know. His younger brother Greg works the farm and lives in the main house. He and a sister Angela are both married with children, your niece and nephews.'

It occurred to Holly that she must check with Detective Norton that her grandparents and their family be told of any new discoveries and investigations into their son's death. Amazingly, she realized their details must surely be on record somewhere if her father's death had been an accident but, having never married, would not be officially connected to her mother. She kept reading.

'Like each of us, my dear, affected by the sudden loss of such a young life and personally feeling my future was torn from my control with his passing, I am not sure John's parents will ever recover from the death of their oldest and beautiful son. They are a close and loving family. I was devastated and don't believe I will ever recover. Sometimes the things we don't want to remember are the hardest to forget.

So I dedicated my life to making you, our child, happy and keeping you safe. I have tried to achieve that but, if not, perhaps my saving grace is to help provide evidence and the true character of Robert Porter. His spirit is dark. Perhaps his targets are innocent symbols of his childhood. Whatever his reasons and motives, we don't need to look much further than such a manipulative person for answers to your father's death.

It was from perhaps a macabre instinct or deep sense of fate, I had your father's DNA test done after he died, needing proof beyond any doubt that he is your father.

With the blessing of his parents, I could never face having John buried so he was cremated and I kept his ashes. They are the contents of the box and yours to deal with and remember as you wish.'

Holly let out a shocked gasp and glanced at the container nearby that she had inherited and retrieved from her mother. Dad?

'Whenever you read this, know that I love you deeply for yourself and being the child gift of the man I was born to love. You are such a treasure to me and a precious symbol of the family we could have created together – John, Rainey and Holly. Mum.'

At the last words, Holly broke down and sobbed, her tears dripping onto the paper in her hands. How could she now not forgive her mother for keeping her father's name secret all these years? The pain she clearly felt and endured at his loss was suffering enough.

Immediately, Holly was struck by a spark of inspiration and similar sense of fate stepping in as that which had clearly haunted Rainey about the DNA test. At the time Rainey's remains were declared ready for release following the autopsy some weeks ago, hesitation and a deep intuition made Holly wait.

Now, after reading the letter, it made the biggest sense that Lorraine Duncan should be cremated, too, and her parents buried together, as it should be and where they belonged.

Only question was where?

Excited, impatient, happy and sad, she needed to phone Tom. Now? She checked her mobile clock. Okay it was late but she would bet he was up waiting for her call when she finished the letter.

Holly pressed his number. The instant he answered before he spoke and because she had waited all her life, she blurted out, 'His name was John Mitchell and I have family.'

Tom didn't say a word for a moment but she would bet he was grinning. 'Never heard you sound happier.'

'The letter is wonderful but sad, too, of course.' She related everything and the amazing news about the contents of the box.

'His ashes?'

'And you know what's even more remarkable? I haven't felt able to bury Mum's remains. Now I realise it's so logical for her to be cremated and my parents buried together.' She drew a breath. 'What do you think?'

'Holly, that's entirely your decision but sounds like a perfect reunion.'

'Doesn't it though? Driving into Melbourne today, I noticed the difference from the life I know here now. Living and working at the roadhouse all these years, I've been welcomed into the warmth and friendliness of country people. Without realizing it was happening, the Wimmera has become my home. My father's roots were in the country. His parents are still there.'

'You sound unsure about something. What's the matter?'

'I'm convinced my parents should be buried together. I just don't know where.'

'Okay,' he said slowly. 'Just a thought but we have a small local cemetery here.'

'We do?'

'It's a ways into the bush. Could give you directions or I could take you out there.'

'Tomorrow?

She heard his low chuckle. 'I'll see if that worker's up for another day shearing.'

With reluctance, Holly sent Gracie a text to come over and wondered if earplugs were an option for the night.

Chapter 12

Next morning, Holly enjoyed the luxury of sleeping in for an extra few minutes after the alarm sounded before rising to start her day. Gracie was nowhere to be seen and must have left early. While still in her cabin, she phoned Detective Norton to provide her father's name and arranged that she and Tom would give their statements late morning.

Walking over to the roadhouse, her steps were light. Tom was due to pick her up after breakfast. Fraser was in custody for his criminal offences. Police re-investigations of three suspicious deaths were in progress. She was about to find a possible resting place for her parents. And she had family.

For the umpteenth time, as she strode into the roadhouse and past the office, Holly paused to offer an unnecessary apology for all her work absences lately.

Gracie waved an arm of dismissal. 'Georgia's loving the money.'

'Pleased I can boost her holiday fund. I should be back in time for the midday shift.'

'With a man like that? Take the day,' Gracie chuckled.

As she served their first customers, Holly wondered what Robert Porter was doing today. His mate was in custody and his own credibility shaky and under review. Personally, she hoped he was freaking out but it was more than mildly troubling he had gone to ground in recent days. His absence was out of character. Yesterday's blunder on Fraser's part must have caused friction. It was now clear from the growing evidence and coincidences between the two that he and Porter worked together. Holly hoped Norton and his team found him soon.

'Sleep okay?' Tom asked as he drew Holly into a kiss before they jumped into his ute later.

'Not too bad. Few restless hours over the anticipation of everything about my new family at the moment.'

'It's a lot to take in.'

'That's for sure. Deep breathing. One day at a time.'

Within minutes, they left the highway and turned onto a gravel road that rose slightly before they turned off into the cemetery. The site was mostly bordered by old sheoaks. A hardy species that tolerated the dry summer climate here, their wispy needle branches attracting rosellas, cockatoos and pink galahs that loved their seed cones.

'It's certainly peaceful,' Holly noticed.

They left the vehicle and began to wander up and down the rows, exploring the large white upright headstones of district pioneers among the shiny grey modern versions. At one point, after they had separated to stroll in different directions, Holly noticed Tom standing for a while before one of the more recent graves. Probably someone he had known.

Joining her again, she glanced up. 'Plenty of German names here. There are a few with your Searle surname. Related?'

'My ancestors. They were early settlers. Probably great great something.'

Holly couldn't get her head around such a long family connection. 'What a precious heritage.'

'There's a family history somewhere on Dad's bookshelves at home.'

'That would be special to have.'

'Might be a subject you could pursue after you meet your grandparents.'

'I could, couldn't I?' The thought appealed to Holly and brightened her mood even more. 'They'll probably have old photos.'

An old climbing rose, gnarled and badly in need of a prune, rambled over a side fence. Deep red geraniums at its base flowered on, regardless of the tough conditions. Gracie had them planted in beds all around the roadhouse for low maintenance and year-round colour alongside local native plants.

Tom approached and reached for her hand. 'What do you think?' His gaze roamed the tranquil site.

'It's perfect. I noticed a brick cremation wall back there near the front fence and gate. I love the rustic name plates inscribed with gold lettering. This place was meant to be. If you hadn't mentioned it, I would never have known about it.'

'Good to go?'

Holly nodded. They drove into town to give their detailed statements at the police station about the roadside incident the day before. It took ages while they were interviewed and questioned. Holly was wary of running into Fraser but she figured by now he had appeared in court and was being held in custody elsewhere in the complex.

Norton brought Holly up to date with Fraser since his arrest. 'He threw the gun out the window somewhere along the highway while he was being pursued. By the time we arrested him, he claimed no weapon. When he made his phone call, looked like he didn't get an answer. He wasn't happy. I bet he tried Porter but he's missing and unreachable. Sounds like he's been dumped. When we questioned Fraser how he knew about the documents, who he's working for, he was uncooperative.

'For now, he's furious at being held. Without Porter's backup, I doubt Fraser has the funds to make bail. Porter's ditched him and on the run so we're hoping Fraser will crack while he's cooling his heels. Give him time to think about his situation.

'Meanwhile, we still have no evidence of a crime against Porter. If we knew he was connected in even the slightest way to your mother's homicide, we could get a court order to stop him leaving the country while we investigate. Word to the wise. Porter could be watching you. Stay sharp and never be alone.'

Holly nodded and blew out an anxious breath of frustration. 'Any idea when this might all be over?'

'Soon. Since Fraser's bungle on the highway, Porter's running scared and probably getting desperate. He's cut himself off from his so-called mate. An ideal tight predicament to make a mistake. We hope he does.'

After giving their statements, Holly and Tom grabbed a late morning café break then headed back out the highway toward home. Tom didn't slow down as they reached the roadhouse but drove right past and kept driving.

'You missed the turn.'

'No I didn't.'

Holly grinned, a budding suspicion building inside her. 'You're kidnapping me?'

'More or less.'

'Where are we going?'

'Home.'

She punched the air. 'Yes!'

Tom laughed. 'Got me a little place down by the Mackenzie River.'

No more than ten minutes later, Holly soon discovered that Tom's *little place* was a spread of hundreds of green acres, dotted with sheep.

'The river runs through the lower paddocks at the bottom of the property. It's actually the boundary between my place and the next property.'

The ute slowed and they turned onto a gravelled avenue lined either side with deciduous trees that looked to be loaded with buds of spring blossom. As they slowly cruised the length of the driveway approach, a peaceful outlook opened up before them. The farmhouse was on a low rise and surrounded by a parkland of eucalypts with views to die for looking down into a valley.

'You're a dark horse,' Holly

murmured. 'This is just lovely.'

'Just the reaction I was hoping for,' Tom confessed almost shyly.

'There's absolutely nothing *not* to like here. Puts my cabin to shame.'

'Nothing wrong with your cabin,' he drawled. 'We've made some awesome memories there.'

They exchanged loaded glances as they pulled up in front of a double garage to one side of the big square home completely surrounded by a veranda. Impatient to explore, Holly scrambled from the vehicle. Solar panels lined part of the roof and a bank of massive rainwater tanks sat a little further out toward the back.

As she turned to absorb the setting below, Tom stood beside her. 'That reedy dam down there actually filters a nearby swamp.'

'Looks to be a magnet for water birds and wildlife.'

'Plenty to watch when you're sitting out on the veranda any time of day. Shall we?'

Holly glanced back toward the house where deeply comfortable chairs beckoned, and nodded. They strolled across to the broad, shallow front steps. Holly nestled into the two-seater and patted the space alongside. Tom joined her, leaning back, arms folded across his chest, legs crossed at the ankles.

'Have you brought other women out here?' she asked softly.

'Nope.'

'Ever been in a long term relationship?'

Holly didn't know why she asked. The thought just came out of nowhere. She knew so little about this man it was hard to know where to start. Apart from mentioning his parents, he never initiated any personal conversation about himself or wider family. At this stage, he remained very much a closed book.

He took a moment to respond and shrugged. 'Not really.'

'Why not?'

'I went wild when I was young. Took a while to mature.'

'Is that why you don't talk about yourself much?'

'Probably. When I finally started to work stuff out, I went to the mines out west. On a generous income, I needed to tough it out for ten years so I could save enough to establish this place.'

Holly turned to him, tucked her feet underneath and nestled closer. 'You've clearly worked hard. Drive rigs. You seem adventurous not wild. Trust me, Tom. Let me in,' she urged softly. 'I really care about you. You jumped feet first into my complicated life and supported me without question. I'd hate anything-'

He leaned forward and pressed a finger to her mouth, replacing it with his lips and a heartbreaking kiss of tenderness.

'I love you more than life itself,' he whispered, 'but I've had to haul myself up by the bootstraps. Occasionally I still have dark days. Is it unfair to ask a woman to endure that?'

'Sorry to hear it but you could have fooled me. You're so considerate and loving. Never seen that side of you.' She paused. 'Besides, we all have good and bad days. Isn't that normal? Seems to me, yours are mostly good, full of lazy humour and a grin I've grown to love. So, thanks for the heads-up but you know I have plenty baggage of my own.'

A brisk wind swept along the veranda, softly whipping strands of rich stunning hair across Holly's face.

Tom gently brushed them aside. 'Might be rain coming. Dad will be antsy if it interrupts shearing. Want to see inside?'

'Absolutely.'

Tom held the front door open. At first sight, Holly's gaze lit on a big freestone fireplace. A random thought crossed her mind that the heirloom clock that had played a significant role in their lives so far would sit perfectly on that long timber mantel.

Embarrassed to be skipping ahead to the possibility of sharing more with Tom, she tore her focus away from the home's main striking feature, to sweep around the deep cosy leather sofas, warm timber floors and, just beyond, a country kitchen to please any chef. Judging by all the pans and utensils hanging up ready to hand, she had to ask.

'Sid would love this. You cook?'

'Only been on my own a few years but I'm slowly learning. So far I've nailed barbeque steak and salad, and sandwiches. Mum writes out the odd recipe for me to try. With a household of men, we just ate whatever she cooked. Now it's only at shearing.'

'To be honest, Sid's amazing and spoils me but over the years, just by watching him and chatting while he's in the roadhouse kitchen, I've picked up some handy tips and basic ideas.'

'Want to see the rest of the place?'

'Yep.'

They moved on through to the other side off a broad rear passageway with a laundry at one end, bedrooms and bathrooms all with great country views. Then Tom wandered into what was clearly his own room. A sumptuous big bed dominated, the space bearing the strong male influence of a man living alone. But the view out the side toward the mountains was exceptional. Holly strolled over, staring through the French windows at the first shower of rain drifting across the property.

Tom wrapped his arms around her from behind. 'Home is wherever I'm with you but I'm hoping you might consider here. For however long we need each other. If I've happened to catch your eye.'

Holly turned into his arms and wrapped her arms around his neck. 'You've had me since I first laid eyes on you.'

'There's no pressure about the future,' he murmured. 'We can take it slow.'

Holly groaned. 'Bugger that. To be honest, I'm fed up with years of simply existing. From now on, I'm going to live my life and take chances. I figure you're a safe bet.'

'Found the right man?' he teased.

'You're the front runner and you know it. The words *stuck with me* come to mind. And even better still, if you introduce me to that lovely big bed behind you, you just might find it impossible to make me leave.'

'So forward,' he pretended to be surprised. 'I like the sound of that.'

As the sky darkened and the rain grew

heavier, layers of winter clothes were cast aside and slithered to the floor. Two warm bodies crushed against each other, learning every dip and curve through touch and slow exploration until they finally tumbled onto the bed.

Lunch seemed unimportant and came much later. Holly woke from a sated sleepy doze to the press of warm lips all over her skin.

'Brought some nibbles and wine. Hungry?'

She stretched, feeling lazy. 'For you, but if food's all you're offering-' She pulled a wry face.

He chuckled. 'Dessert comes after.'

'I love promises.'

They sat up in bed together, pulled the doona around them and indulged in snacks, Holly drinking a luscious rosé and Tom opting for his usual beer.

Feeling more secure in their new, deeper relationship, she prompted, 'Are you going to tell me what happened?' Their conversation earlier out on the veranda on arrival had been cut short but he understood what she meant.

'Kids growing up on farms learn how to drive when they can barely see over the dashboard and through the windscreen. Mates and I all pretty much got our licence and secondhand utes at eighteen.

'A few of my friends surrendered to the pressure of drinking, especially the footy stars. They were hero-worshipped, young and feeling bulletproof. My closest mate got hooked hard. I tried talking to him but he wouldn't listen, bagged me, told me to loosen up. All I could do was watch out for him and not be too obvious about it. He was an angry drunk.

'Last night of his life, he was wasted at a campfire in the bush. I offered to drive him home, even stole his keys until he found out and thumped me. Knocked me out for a bit. By the time I came to, he was gone. Apparently none of our mates tried to stop him or went with him.

'I asked them what direction he headed and went searching for him. Hardest thing I ever had to face was finding his vehicle slammed into a tree and split in half. And so much blood. Wish I felt different but, even to this day, I can't stop blaming myself.'

Holly reflected on the coincidence of Tom's mate and her father both being victims of road accidents. 'This morning I saw you standing for a while by a grave. Was that his?'

Tom nodded.

'What was his name?' Somehow it seemed important to acknowledge the existence of a lost friend.

'Andy. Andy MacDonald.' Holly could see him struggling with his emotions. 'He was an only child.'

She groaned in heartache both for Tom and Andy's family.

'At Andy's funeral, his folks thanked me for going to find him. Told me they knew he had problems, tried to help him and no one was to blame.'

'Generous of them in the circumstances.'

'Yeah. Took away a small corner of my guilt but I still battled demons for years.'

'Did you have counselling?'

'Eventually.' He pulled a wry grin. 'Mum nagged.'

'That why you've encouraged me to talk out my own grief?'

He nodded.

Without saying a word, Holly set her wine aside and hugged him, nestling her head into his neck. 'Tragedy comes to most people. We'll never be the same but we have to go on living. Only purpose I can understand why is perhaps because we survived for a reason.'

'Thanks for the gentle nudge,' he whispered. 'I've never had the courage to tell anyone else except the counsellor.'

'Maybe that's why we were drawn to

each other. Two lonely aching souls.' When he stayed silent, she murmured, 'Moving on, you promised me dessert.'

'So I did.'

Turned out, it was even better than the first course. When the rain eased and rays of thin sunshine broke through the scudding clouds, they forced themselves back to reality. Standing on the veranda waiting for Tom to collect something from the house before they left, Holly stared across the paddocks to the creek. She heard the front door shut behind her.

At her side, he handed her a huge box. 'If you're going to be my woman, you'll need a pair of boots.'

Holly's expression broke into a smile and she laughed. 'You didn't.'

'Can't stride around a farm in those,' he glanced down at her favourite sneakers and shook his head. 'Doesn't look right for a country girl when you're wearing jeans.'

She lifted the lid to reveal long boots. 'You know my size and had them made! They're gorgeous.' Holly ran her hands over the smooth tooled leather.

'Colour is called *cognac*. Figured that was appropriate.'

Holly chuckled. 'They're perfect in every way. They match my hair.' She hugged and kissed him then put them on and paraded along the veranda.

'Damn you look good, woman,' Tom said.

Back at the roadhouse later, Holly accepted a lingering goodbye from Tom who was heading over to his parents' property to check on the interruption to shearing for the day. She felt like a different woman from the one who had left this morning.

As she strode into the restaurant, she checked her watch and said to Alice, 'You're still working.'

Alice shrugged. 'Rain stopped shearing for a bit so Ted picked up the kids.'

'I can take over now if you want.'

'Okay. Thanks. I'll finish up my orders first then it's all yours.'

Gracie breezed in from out the back. 'You're looking pleased with yourself.'

'It's the boots.' Holly extended a leg.

'They're smart,' Gracie agreed, arms folded across her ample chest, her keen gaze assessing, 'but I think it's a little more than footwear.'

She sighed in resignation. 'You may be old but you're wise. Tom took me to the farm.'

'So, you two got together?'

'Don't make it sound so impossible.'

'Was beginning to think so. You both

danced around it long enough. Like, two years of sparking off each other before anyone made a move. That's slow in anyone's language.'

'We might,' Holly conceded slowly.

'I knew it. About time. I must tell Sid.'

'Actually, no. He needs to hear it from me. Now I know about my father and after all the years Sid kind of stepped into the role of a favourite uncle, I don't want him to feel he's been replaced in my heart.'

'Of course. That's a touching sentiment.'

After Alice left, Holly took over the remainder of her shift for the day. Before heading over to her cabin for the night, she loitered in the kitchen. Sid was scrubbing down, the long white apron he wore over his tropical shirt showing evidence of another busy day, flat cap tugged low over his face.

'Did you get everything done today that you needed?' he asked.

'We did. I never knew about the local cemetery. I want my parents to be buried there together. It felt like such a special place.'

'Hope it brings you closure, Sunshine,' he murmured, one of the rare times his expression included a frown. 'You deserve it.'

'Thanks. Can I ask you a personal question?'

'If I said no, it wouldn't stop you.'

'True. Why didn't you ever marry? I know getting married isn't a law or anything but its tradition and most people do. You're a cool guy. No one ever wanted to snap you up?'

Sid grinned and stopped cleaning. 'You know Gracie and I were children of hippies. Not interested in the quarter acre block and mortgage. Our folks were always their own boss, never worked for anyone else. But they always made friends wherever they went. Guess my sister and I inherited the freedom of a simple life and that love of being with people, usually in a small community. We had lovers and partners at various times but nothing long term. One or the other ended it for whatever reason and moved on. Never consciously sought any permanent relationship. Why do you ask?'

'Because I think I've found that someone for me.'

'Know who that would be,' he said softly.

Holly smiled. 'Any advice?'

'Best I know from my own experience is to live like tomorrow isn't coming and yesterday never happened. Just be happy, Sunshine.'

'After all the upheaval lately, I'm

actually beginning to believe I will be.'

Sid sauntered around the long kitchen island and they hugged.

'I know the fate of my mother now,' she faltered, fighting back rising emotions, 'and you know I've just learned the identity of my father. I'm a creation of their love and hold part of each of them inside me.

'But you're a whole other special person to me in your own right with an entirely separate role in my life. You're the father figure I didn't have and so desperately needed. Offering your support in every way when you barely knew me. I hope you realise that and I need you to hear it from me. Just so you know, your role is ongoing, okay? You'll never be replaced in my life.'

Sid and Gracie were happy souls, endlessly giving to customers and travellers for decades but Holly's words cracked him up. Speechless, he simply grabbed her in a bear hug then turned away and continued scouring his kitchen. A big man with a big heart in every sense of the word.

Stepping from the roadhouse out into the night, she paused for a moment to take in the starry evening. The rain clouds had long gone, blessing the earth with a damp freshness.

She would call Tom before she went to

sleep but he knew tonight was for reflection. Of all that had happened to her in recent months, and all that still needed to be arranged and done.

For the two people who were the reason she existed and stood here alone, but not lonely.

For the future, what it might look like and who might be by her side.

Chapter 13

In her cabin later, Holly called Tom and shared her anxiety about contacting her Mitchell grandparents. 'Now I know about them, I'm keen to at least reach out and make contact. It's daunting not knowing how I might be received.'

'Don't let uncertainty hold you back. Just do it. Make the call.'

'Okay. In the morning, after the breakfast rush.'

Holly decided she needed to be more informed about the Mitchell family and her father's background before speaking to her grandparents. She opened both his birth and death certificates. *John Anderson Mitchell, parents Paul Edward Mitchell and Carol May nee Anderson. Born 1968, Daylesford Victoria.* Which would be the nearest town to where his parents still lived on their family farm. On the death certificate, much of the information was similar. *John Anderson Mitchell,* his parents, and the addition of siblings, *Gregory and Angela Mitchell,* plus his home address in the city and occupation, *Lawyer.*

Holly had hoped for more detail but, although the certificates contained the basics, at least it had started to bring him to life in her mind. To prepare for tomorrow's phone call, she looked up her grandparents' landline number and address. Then checked the Maps app on her phone to see how far away. From the roadhouse, it was actually only about a two hour drive down the highway then across country toward Daylesford. Who knew her father's family had always lived so close?

Next morning on her way past Gracie's office, she mentioned her intention to call the Mitchell family and forced herself to push through the early shift in the restaurant with Sophie until Alice arrived, then took a break.

In her cabin for privacy, her heart pounding with anxiety, Holly held her mobile and pressed her grandparents' number. As it rang out, she almost hung up.

Then a bright older female voice answered. 'Hello?'

Feeling awkward, Holly asked, 'Is this Carol Mitchell?'

'Speaking. Who's calling?'

'This is Holly, Rainey Duncan's daughter.'

Holly thought she heard a faint gasp and the line went silent on the other end for long seconds. To fill the space, she said, 'Do you know who I am?'

'Oh my dear,' the voice had grown shaky, 'yes, I know exactly who you are.'

Holly was surprised to hear it but also pleased because now, hopefully, this conversation would be easier. A positive at least and not too scary after all, although her heart still raced with apprehension. 'Do you mind if we talk for a moment?'

'Can you hold on? I'll get Paul and put this handset on loud speaker so we can both hear you.'

'Of course.' Holly heard the phone set down and Carol calling out for her husband, faint conversation in the background then shuffling as the phone was picked up again.

'Holly?'

'Yes I'm here.'

'Paul and I are listening. After Lorraine disappeared we had no way of getting in touch with you. Your mother was always so cautious, even afraid. She contacted us but we had no phone number or address for her. We briefly saw and held you, Holly, as a baby. Over the years, Lorraine wrote us letters enclosing photographs of you. We watched you growing up but not in person.'

So her mother had stayed in touch with the Mitchells but kept the two families apart. Believing it would maintain everyone's safety. And it almost did.

'I never knew.' Holly's eyes filled with tears of joy. 'I've only just learned about my father.'

'Oh my dear, it's so lovely to speak to you and hear your voice.'

'Thank goodness. I was so nervous before I called.'

'I can imagine but there's no need. Trust us, this is very special to speak to you. You're our oldest grandchild. The others call us Gramps and Granny. We'd love it if you would, too. When you're ready. I know it will feel strange.'

Holly smiled to herself and swiped at her damp cheeks. 'Okay.' Now came the hard part. 'You've probably heard in the news that my mother's body was found recently and her cause of death established as a homicide.' She found it harsh and difficult even voicing such a reality.

'Yes, dear. We were devastated and so anxious as to how all this was affecting you. Are you all right?'

'I'm managing, thanks. I have close friends and support. You would have been shocked, too. The reason I discovered my father's name and family is because I have only just found a key which my mother left for me. It related to letters she had written and left in a bank security vault for me just before she died.' Holly felt it best not to mention the box just yet and what it contained. 'I've only just opened and read them. I might just warn you to prepare yourself for what I have to say.'

'All right. We're listening.'

'One letter of my mother was detailed and brought out new information and background on a man she knew at the same time as my … your son, John. Robert Porter.'

'Oh yes, indeed. Lorraine mentioned Porter and warned us about him. And, please, refer to John as your father. You must. It will help and he would have loved you dearly.'

Holly swallowed back tears. 'Would he?'

'Your father was so over the moon at the news Lorraine was expecting you. Thank heavens there's less stigma for single mothers these days. You were conceived in love and that's not a crime. You were to be our first grandchild. We met your mother often when she was dating John and could see the relationship was serious and genuine, that marriage was ahead. John adored Lorraine. They suited so well together. Because of your mother's deep sense of privacy, John talked about moving to live in the country after they married. Set up a local law practice here. Oh, if only-'

Holly heard the ache of sadness in Carol's voice. 'Of course Porter was the reason for Lorraine keeping a certain distance from our family in case it led to harm,' Carol continued. 'It was a wrench to not see you both but we understood and respected her wishes and concerns. Especially after losing your father.'

'I've handed over Mum's letter to Detective Norton who is leading the reopened investigation. I've asked him to keep you up to date with anything new that comes to light.'

'Thank you, dear. That means so much.'

'I didn't understand the possible connection between my mother's disappearance and death, and my father's road accident, until Mum's letter.' Holly paused. This was going to be difficult for them to hear and process. 'A certain level of doubt and suspicion surrounds Porter now since the background knowledge given in Mum's letter. Not proof exactly but grounds for further investigation. The police think he might be linked with not only his first wife's death but my father's death, too.'

Holly heard a gasp in the background

from Carol then Paul spoke for the first time. 'Good heavens!'

'I know. It's a lot to take in, isn't it? Sometimes I feel so angry but also optimistic by everything that's slowly unfolding.'

'We all suffered so much over the tragedy of John's death,' Carol's thin voice came on the line again. 'At the time, all I remember is that life became utterly overwhelming. He was always such a careful driver. That he should just run off the road and crash for no reason seemed unbelievable. And now you're saying there's some doubt?'

'Possibly,' Holly was quick to explain without too much further alarm.

As Carol seemed to be distressed with emotion, Paul took up the conversation. 'Lorraine came to us, Holly, after John died. About his burial. We struggled with her request because it was a difficult situation for everyone. But after consulting with Greg and Angela, we all agreed Lorraine and her child would have been John's future and become part of our family.

'We gave your mother permission for his cremation and to keep his ashes. So we just held a private local memorial service for John, which Lorraine attended of course. In hindsight, it was for the best. We were all in shock and it was as much as we could cope with at the time. I don't know how Lorraine continued on after that.'

'Judging by what she wrote in her letters I don't believe she did and she worried for you both as well. And I'm pleased you mentioned what happened after my father's death because, actually,' she hesitated, 'I have his ashes in a box with me now. That was also left in the bank safety deposit box for me by Mum.'

'He's never been buried anywhere?' Carol spoke again.

'No. Sounds like Mum couldn't deal with it at the time. To be honest, maybe she wanted to keep him with her. I never knew any of this until her recent letters. And that's another thing. Now that Mum has been found and the autopsy completed, I can have her burial. Since I'm in possession of my father's ashes, I felt Mum should be cremated, too, and my parents buried together. What do you think?'

'That's your decision to make,' Paul said, 'but it sounds a lovely idea.' His voice cracked a little in reaction to the suggestion.

'There's a small peaceful cemetery near where I've lived in recent years at the Coach Roadhouse on the highway. I've met someone,' she said carefully, 'and I believe my future might be in the area, so I was thinking to have a memorial service for them both and the burial out there. If you agree, I feel you should be there, too.'

'When would that be, Holly?' Carol asked.

'As soon as I can arrange it.'

'We're shearing at the moment,' Paul said, 'but as soon as that's done.'

'Tom's helping his father shearing, too,' Holly rattled off without thinking.

'Tom?' Carol latched onto the accidental hint. 'Is he the *someone* you mentioned?'

'Yes.'

'We're happy for you, Holly. We hope all goes well with your young man. Just let us know when you're having the service and our family will be there.'

'Of course.'

'Your uncle and aunt, Greg and Angela, and all your nieces and nephews will be so excited to hear about your call. You must come out to the farm. See where your father grew up. We have so many albums of photos to share with you. We wouldn't want you to feel overwhelmed but we have so many questions about your life, too.'

Holly smiled to herself. 'That's fine. I look forward to catching up with everyone out there after the formalities are over.'

'Wonderful.' She heard the warmth in Carol's voice. 'Bring Tom if you like.'

After they hung up, Holly sat in stunned reflection and her head spun. It seemed almost surreal and too easy how naturally a connection was established with her grandparents. And of course in hindsight, she had worried over nothing at all. Helped by the fact that her mother had maintained an open communication over the years with the Mitchell family. For which, as it turned out, she was now so grateful. Perhaps that had been the bottom line reason for her mother's caution after all.

Holly had been completely unaware that her mother kept in touch with her father's family and could have been regretful, even angry, at the overdue news but as Granny Carol had so tactfully said, she respected Rainey's decision.

Holly suddenly realized the time. Her lunch break was over but before she resumed her shift in the restaurant, she needed to see Gracie.

'You're smiling so it must have gone well,' her boss said as she entered the office.

'I don't believe I've ever had an easier conversation with strangers.' Filled with enthusiasm, Holly related the gist of the three-way chat with her grandparents.

Gracie slowly shook her head and covered Holly with the compassionate gaze that, over time, she had grown to understand meant love. 'If there's any rainbow and sunshine after the past dark years of your life, it must surely be knowing you have family out there.'

'I know it. Out of grief and tragedy I'm feeling blessed with the most exciting hope for what lies ahead. But just because a whole new world has opened up for me with the Mitchells and Tom, I still need and want you to be part of it, too.'

Gracie chuckled. 'Girl, you'd have a hard time getting rid of me. Sid and I aren't going anywhere anytime soon so consider this another one of the many homes you'll have to choose from in the future. I expect you to bring me all the babies you're going to have with Tom so I can have lots of cuddles.'

'Gracie! You're getting way ahead of yourself.'

She waved an arm, enjoying the teasing. 'You two were made for each other. Bit slow out of the starting gate though.'

Holly rolled her eyes. 'Actually, with the police investigation, getting in touch with the Mitchells and growing closer to Tom lately, I feel like fate has stepped in to decide for me and the time is right now. I need your help with arranging my parents' memorial service. Do you mind?'

'Course not. How about we all have a round table together tonight after one of Sid's roast dinners and work it all out?'

'Thanks. You're the best.'

'I know.' Gracie laughed and waved her away.

Holly wondered if she imagined glistening moisture in the steadfast eyes of the woman who had so readily gathered her into the roadhouse fold.

So that evening, Holly, Gracie and Sid began dealing with the emotional reality of organizing a fitting tribute for her mother's cremation and parents' burial together. The most difficult task, however, was sitting down to begin writing her own personal eulogy of her mother's life for the coming memorial service.

As the day approached, Holly grew concerned that, since all of the roadhouse employees and many district people had indicated they would be attending, who would keep the roadhouse open?

Having lived and worked in the country now for years, she should have known that if you want something done in the country, the phone tree works miracles. Community leaders had already organised a roadhouse team. CWA ladies manning the restaurant service, a couple of local district cooks manning Sid's kitchen.

Georgia's little sister, Sally, was delighted on two fronts. Not only did it mean a day off school but she had passed the working age threshold by a matter of weeks. The nervously excited girl took charge of the checkout in the mini market after some lessons in the days beforehand from Reilly. Watching the two young people working together, Holly wondered if she imagined some sparks of attraction in the air between the teens.

A few days before the planned memorial services, Lorraine Duncan's cremation in a private Ballarat chapel was an intimate service Holly barely managed but for the support of Tom and her closest friends and family. Holly dug deep to hold herself together as the huge emotional load pressed in upon her. With Tom by her side, she allowed the process of grief and closure to take its course. Sid and Gracie too, as always, stayed close.

Her mother's dearest friend, Susan Rogers, arrived from the city and met them in Ballarat and would be staying overnight in a roadhouse cabin when they returned home later. Despite the intervening years, she and Holly instantly recognised each other, warmly hugged and smiled through tears.

The Mitchell family arrived in two four wheel drives. As they stepped from their vehicles, the fact that Holly was the only redhead among a crowd of blondes, she found mildly amusing, even in the solemn circumstances. Meeting her grandparents, Greg and Angela and their partners for the first time was stirring in every way. For Holly, being introduced and embraced one at a time, added a depth of meaning and support to an already challenging occasion.

Seeing Greg looking so much like the photograph of her father, and Paul an older version of the man John Mitchell may have become with age, wrenched Holly's heart in the best and worst ways.

The most significant person Holly wanted to attend, although distanced from investigations since that first fateful day, was prospector Benny Wade who found a discarded mobile phone in the bush which triggered the discovery of so much more than anyone could ever have imagined.

Scrubbed up, his beard trimmed and looking respectfully smart in an old black checked suit, Holly hugged the elderly man at first sight. The ripple effect of ongoing consequences since his find that day which had already involved and touched so many people's lives could not have been predicted.

For the actual interment and memorial services two days later, the early spring morning dawned overcast with light misty rain, which soon cleared, chased by a lively breeze.

Holly rummaged among her mother's belongings to find the favourite pearl and marcasite brooch inherited from Grandma Duncan that Rainey often wore. She pinned it on the lapel of her denim jacket worn over a black maxi dress, her new boots peeping out beneath. Only when she had also tucked a photo of her father into her pocket did she feel ready.

As they arrived at the cemetery, it was to find cars were parked in every possible space outside in the surrounding bush among trees. Mourners stepped from their cars over damp grass. The crowd included friends, workmates and family. Behind, stood a row of uniformed police, among them Detective Norton, Ewan Holt and Louise Casey. Holly recognised so many local district faces come to pay their respects for a woman they never knew but who had lost her life in their home country and whose daughter they had embraced into their community.

She caught sight of Billie Gibbs with Noah Sutton and also two other couples. Addie Kendall with her fiancé Harry Chandler together with Piper Thorne and Ben Powell who had detoured from their motorhome travels to be here. Holly had come to know all three women as they passed through the Coach Roadhouse often over the years.

Casting her gaze about as she, Tom, Sid and Gracie walked toward the memorial wall where the small ceremony was to take place, Holly was emotionally gripped by the nature of the day.

As a result of her mother's tragic disappearance nearby all those years ago, all the people here today were her family, in reality and by association. Made up of those who loved her and were a precious part of her life, and all the many warm hearted country people she had come to know as they passed through the roadhouse doors.

There was no specific service or protocol for the interment of ashes. The local minister, robes flying in the wind, led a warm and simple service with prayers, a poem she had chosen and a reading. Then her parents' ashes were slid into their niche in the memorial wall. Together. Where they should be at long last.

After the ceremony, Holly stood for

a moment, head bowed and whispered a prayer of her own. *For those who loved me, even before I was born and in return who are loved as much. No matter how deep you sleep, nothing will keep your spirits from running freely in my heart. You are both at peace now. You will be with me in the sun, the wind and the rain. I will remember and love you both forever.*

Emotionally drained but calm, Holly murmured to Tom, 'Always a bad idea to wear mascara to a funeral.'

He gently brushed the tears from her cheeks.

The simple ceremony had barely finished when the few remaining clouds parted, bathing the cemetery and the mourners in gentle sunshine.

As people hugged Holly and the Mitchell family, she noticed Detective Norton step aside to answer his phone then beckon to Ewan and Louise who followed, all immediately leaving together in their official car. Police business never stops, Holly thought idly, and didn't think any more of it.

Everyone moved back toward the highway and the small weatherboard community church for a short celebration of life service. Even more people gathered, filling the pews to overflowing, many standing at the rear. Vases of cascading flower arrangements, abundant with the first spring blooms and blossom, dotted the interior, beautifully done by local ladies. Sunbeams streamed through the stained glass windows, casting coloured shafts of light over everyone.

Holly thought it the most uplifting sight as though her parents, now safely in their final resting place, had opened a door to a new world and life of possibilities that lay ahead, with so many wonderful family and friends.

The service in honour of her parents was filled with songs of praise and eulogies read by Greg Mitchell for his brother, John, and Sid at Holly's request on behalf of her mother.

Holly hoped all those in attendance, after hearing the words spoken by two strong male voices echo around the church, would know her parents, the two people so dear to her heart, a little better. Even though she never knew her father, through her mother's letter and old photographs as well as previous conversations and more to come with the Mitchell family, she was learning more about him.

Feeling calmly comforted as the organist played Amazing Grace, offering its message of peace, Holly took a deep breath and walked from the church alongside Tom.

As always, the church hall next door offered a generous country lunch and a more casual atmosphere after an emotional morning. As Holly tried to grab something to eat and balance a mug of tea, she didn't recall ever being so warmly hugged. Accompanied by smiles and kind words, she also felt the deepest sense of belonging.

The day's sadness was eased by chatting with her father's family, learning more about them all, with promises to go visit the Mitchell farm soon. Holly trusted today's services offered them the opportunity to grieve together but also provided the beginnings of closure. In the circumstances, so important for them all. Because her Duncan grandparents were no longer alive, Holly knew having Paul and Carol in her life was doubly precious.

Later, Tom grabbed her hand and led her through the crowd to introduce his parents, Allan and Meg.

'We've heard a lot about you, young lady,' Allan chuckled.

'Because I've dragged him away from shearing?' Holly smiled. She recognised them from occasional visits to the roadhouse but, amid all that had happened of late, hadn't made the connection.

'With good reason,' Meg assured her.

Then followed an invitation to visit another farm. Soon. To meet Tom's brothers, Stephen and Jordan, absent today with apologies to manage the end of shearing. Holly was swiftly growing to understand she was destined to be a true country woman. Probably for life. And she wouldn't have had it any other way.

Suddenly, Billie Gibbs sidled up beside her and linked arms. 'District grapevine has your *relationship* well and truly sorted. A certain man with his arm around your waist. Hardly leaving your side.'

'Made it a bit obvious, did he?'

'He's gorgeous, you lucky lady.' Billie turned aside. 'Do you remember Noah?'

'I do now.' They shook hands.

'He's finished renovating the old homestead and I'm fast learning about gardening.'

'You're engaged and married!' Holly only just noticed the rings.

Billie beamed. 'He was taking too long so *I* asked *him*! We had stones from his mother and grandmother's rings made into a heritage ring of our own.'

'It's lovely. Congratulations.' She hugged them both.

'We've brought more friends you'll recognise.'

Addie Kendall stepped forward, her long hair caught back in a thick braid, a delicate sparkly ring on her left hand. One very handsome fiancé, Harry, alongside.

They hugged. 'Haven't seen you at the Coach in a while,' Holly said.

'We've been travelling overseas in the European summer,' Addie said.

'Getting to know each other's habits. Good and bad.' Harry smiled.

'Our tree paddock is still waiting for us to put a house on it,' Addie said. 'Haven't definitely decided what we want our family home to look like yet but we're thinking some sort of passive solar eco structure.'

'Good for you. Lots of work ahead.'

Then Holly caught sight of attractive and bubbly Piper Thorne and her partner Ben Powell. Yet again, she was hugged tight. 'Where have you travelled from?'

'Turned around and headed south from further north up the east coast.' Piper frowned. 'We would have come from anywhere to be with you today.'

'Thank you,' Holly whispered. 'You're all such awesome friends.' She glanced around the group and they all made promises to keep in touch.

The gathering dwindled and people gradually slipped away back to their lives. The CWA ladies cleaned up in the kitchen, boxing up leftovers for Holly. As Tom carted the food out to his ute, Gracie appeared by her side.

'Hate to introduce reality,' she said quietly, 'but Porter's still missing.'

'It's okay,' Holly assured her. 'I'm going back to the farm with Tom. I'll be fine. Lots to process and discuss after today.'

'Of course. Don't rush back to work. See you whenever.'

They hugged.

Exhausted on all fronts, Holly barely registered the drive to the farm. Tom stowed the food in the fridge while she took a hot shower and reappeared in a fluffy robe.

A glass of wine sat waiting on the kitchen bench. Lost, she took it out onto the veranda, the day's warmth fading with the setting sun to find Tom already had the same idea so she snuggled against him on the seat. His arm went around her shoulder. In peaceful silence they watched the daylight slowly dissolve, to be overtaken by the first stars.

'One day at a time,' he murmured.

'Exactly.' She paused. 'It's so lovely here.'

'I'm hoping you'll share it with me. For life,' he whispered.

It was the most timely and appropriate moment. Holly's eyes flooded with tears of happiness. She couldn't respond. But she figured the long passionate kiss they shared was probably answer enough.

They were about to move indoors and seal their commitment when Holly's mobile buzzed in her robe pocket. She had forgotten to switch it from silent.

'It's Detective Norton.' She flicked the phone to speaker.

After a quick preliminary greeting, Norton said, 'Holly, we have a break in your mother's case.'

Holly glanced at Tom as she asked, 'What happened?'

'Basically, we're in plea negotiations with Fraser,' Norton said. 'He's talking. I know you've had a tough day and it's getting late but we'd like to bring you up to speed. If you feel up to it, I can come out to the roadhouse now or call first thing in the morning.'

'Oh, I won't sleep a wink until I hear more.' Holly mouthed *Okay?* to Tom and he nodded. 'I'm at Tom's farm. Know it?'

'We'll find you. Be there shortly.'

When she hung up, Holly stared at Tom. On a personal high only moments before, she was now swiftly plunged back into a familiar reality. 'I guess I should get dressed.'

Thirty minutes later, Detective Norton and Ewan Holt arrived. Tom had lit a match to the open fire against the early spring night's chill and boiled the kettle while Holly slipped into comfortable pull-ons, a windcheater and brushed her damp hair.

Tom ushered the officers into the living room. Once settled with hot drinks and leftover home baked goodies from today's lunch, Norton explained.

'Since Fraser couldn't contact Porter or make bail after the highway incident, he's been sweating in custody. He had a visitor earlier today. We're guessing possibly sent by Porter. Judging by the tense conversation, I'd say Fraser got spooked because he just offered to cooperate.'

'Is that why you left the cemetery?' Holly asked.

Norton nodded. 'Seems Porter has not only abandoned Fraser but probably also tossed out a threat through the visitor to keep his mouth shut. Meanwhile he's disappeared and left Fraser to take the possible blame for three suspicious deaths. He claims the offences were committed under pressure. All started in their teens. Porter dealt with some trouble Fraser got into. Handled it and covered it up. So Fraser owed him. Porter basically blackmailed him but paid well and never let the little guy forget about the *favour* he did in the past. Porter was the mastermind and orchestrated the planning. Fraser carried it out. Porter was always far away with a clear alibi. Fraser took all the risks.

'In Linda Porter's case, she came from money. Because she refused to drop divorce proceedings, Porter convinced

Fraser to setup their house to make it look like the wife was negligent by leaving the gas on. Fraser flicked the match and triggered a fire. Took a while but because Linda Porter's death was eventually declared accidental, Porter was paid out for both Linda's life insurance and the house insurance.'

Looking directly at Holly with compassion, Norton hesitated. 'In your father's case, Fraser claims his car accident was only ever intended to be a warning for him to stay away from your mother. Fraser tampered with the tyres, caused a blow out, vehicle swerved off the road and crashed.'

Holly felt breathless with horror, as if she had been punched directly in the heart. She wanted to feel anger but grew numb. The depth of the cruelty inflicted on multiple innocent people by this pair of criminals, defied all of her belief in humanity. A harmless wife seeking to escape; a man whose only crime was to love her mother. Norton had yet to explain the last one which she already knew would be the hardest truth she would ever have to face.

Aware Norton was closely watching her emotions, he continued. 'This is the first evidence John Mitchell's death was directly linked to Porter and Fraser. The little guy had no need to even admit his complicity. At the time, there was no clear evidence identified of mechanical interference. I'd say Fraser's conscience has finally kicked in and his options have run out. He's seriously mad at Porter. Looking for payback on his so-called mate's desertion. Big time.'

Norton paused and steadily held Holly's gaze for the longest time, as if assessing whether to continue. Knowing what was to come, she said quietly, 'Keep going. Please.'

'Are you sure?'

She nodded, not convinced at all but needing to hear. For her mother's sake and her own peace of mind.

'Fraser's account was detailed,' he warned. 'The short version?'

Holly shook her head. Norton's job was dealing with the harsher side of life but Holly braced herself and stared at the floor, determined to persevere. She had endured so much. This final anguish to learn the truth must be borne or she would forever wonder.

'Fraser tracked your mother from Melbourne to her last stop at the roadhouse,' Norton continued. 'He went on ahead to a bush track turn off before she was due to reach the B&B. He parked his vehicle then went out onto the side of the highway to watch and wait for her approach. Since it was late afternoon but still daylight, Fraser gambled on Rainey's humanity and profession as a nurse to help. When he flagged her down, she stopped.

'He told Rainey his ute wouldn't start. Claimed he'd been having battery trouble. Knew he should have recharged it. That his mate was injured in the bush and with no phone reception, just needed her vehicle to either use jumper leads he had in his ute to try and get it started or to take him and his imaginary mate into Horsham hospital. He argued it would be quicker than an ambulance. Your mother agreed.'

'Of course she would.' As she listened to Norton's words, Holly couldn't help but visualise every single one of her mother's last moments alive.

'Fraser jumped into her vehicle and guided her along the bush track. When they reached the ute, Rainey suggested she check on his mate to see the extent of the injuries. If it was serious, they would head straight to hospital. Otherwise she would help get his ute started and he could take his mate into town himself. Fraser pointed further into the bush to indicate where his mate was supposed to be while he lied about getting a medical kit from his ute. Instead, he grabbed a rock, crept up and struck her on the head from behind.'

Holly drew in a horrified gasp and put her hands over her face.

Norton's voice lowered and softened. 'You okay?'

She nodded.

'He claimed Porter told him just to give her a warning. Was going to rough her up then leave her. From questions Rainey asked of Porter, he guessed she was onto him and needed her to back off. But after Fraser's nasty blow, your mother fell to the ground and never moved again. Fraser panicked of course. Swore it was never meant to happen, dug a shallow grave and buried her.

'When I asked him about the phone, he said it must have slipped from your mother's pocket because she fell suddenly and heavily. Fraser didn't notice it. Sounded annoyed when he said if he had, she would probably never have been found. That it was just dumb luck the old prospector located it with his metal detector.'

As simmering rage at Fraser's callous reaction rose inside her and appalling images flashed across her mind at the shocking scene that played out in the bush, a missing piece of information rose in Holly's mind. 'What happened to Mum's car?'

'Good question,' Norton agreed. 'We asked. He sold it to a dodgy mate to completely strip it down. Might have been too risky to take a perfectly good vehicle to a crusher. Questions possibly asked, unless they put some dents in it to make it look like it had been in an accident.'

Holly sank back onto the sofa, one of Tom's arms around her all the time and, with a shaky hand, accepted the brandy he offered. Her mind was a mess, anger and grief ripping through her body.

'Fraser's also given us a lead on the money trail. To pay Fraser, apparently Porter siphoned cash from his employer's business. It went through company accounts, not personal. We're following that up. So on a totally positive note, Fraser's admissions mean we have enough evidence now to arrest Porter and stop him absconding overseas. We've had a watch on him. Nothing so far at ports and airports, so he's still in the country. Which also means he's still around,' Norton said pointedly to Holly.

'I'll make sure she's never alone,' Tom said.

'Good man. Eyes-on at all times and we'll have our own man watching you 24/7. Fraser's confessions have helped open the way to solving three suspicious deaths. But we still need Porter. We're close, Holly. He's gone underground but we'll get him.'

'I hope it's soon,' Holly said. 'So what does Fraser's plea deal mean?'

'Pleads guilty to lesser charges. Reduced sentence. No need for a trial but still means a long spell in prison. Because homicides are involved, bail's automatically refused so Fraser stays in custody.

'And Porter, too, when we arrest him. Fraser's given us background on Porter. Poor family, tough childhood. Became obsessed with money and used his charms on women to gain access to whatever they had. Motive was jealousy for your father which turned into revenge. And profit for Linda Porter who stood to inherit wealth, and your mother who benefited from the sale of her family home. It was no coincidence that Porter came back into your mother's life about that time. In each case, different scenarios but for a common purpose. Crimes of opportunity that became personal when your mother began to suspect him.'

'User,' Holly muttered.

'I have a hunch about Porter. Don't be alarmed but he knows that, now your mother's been found, her estate can be settled and you inherit. My gut's telling me you're a potential target for blackmail. He'll need you alive for that. So, like I said, stay alert.' Norton rose. 'We'll keep you posted and let me know if you have the smallest suspicion about *anything*. Meanwhile, stay safe.'

'Thank you.'

With the weight of Norton's potential warning of trouble and tonight's revelations churning over in her mind after he left, Holly was silent for a long time staring into the fire.

'You should go to bed,' Tom murmured beside her.

'Who can sleep?' she groaned. 'What are the odds of the best and worst things happening on the same day in your life?'

'Slim.'

What should have been the joy of their future together was eclipsed by Norton's disclosures.

'How about we just snuggle under the covers anyway and I hold you?'

'Okay,' she whispered, rising, arms around each other.

'I love you, Holly.' Tom kissed the top of her head.

'I love you, too.' She began to cry.

It was barely daylight when Holly woke from a disturbed sleep of nightmares. Tom had held her tight and even now his warm protective body was wrapped around her. She frowned in annoyance, aware something had disturbed her but fuzzy about exactly what. Then she heard it again. Her phone buzzing on the bedside table. She almost ignored it but her conscience intruded. It might be more news from Norton although what else he could possibly have to tell her, she found hard to imagine.

Unfolding herself gently so as not to disturb Tom, Holly sat up and reached for her mobile, frowning, not recognizing the anonymous number. Didn't matter. They'd left a message. Why would a stranger do that? She pushed a hand through her tumble of thick hair, her mind still fuzzy from lack of sleep and sobbing grief.

When she read the text, her heartbeat quickened. It was perfectly plain who sent it. The past twelve hours had sprung yet another surprise. She wondered if he was nearby and how he had tapped into her number. These days, apparently easy enough, especially if you were a criminal.

Holly hesitated. Looking down at Tom sleeping beside her, regretful that such a beautiful man was dragged into all this. Should she wake him or leave him sleep and slip out alone, just meet the guy as he demanded? Norton was having her followed. She would be safe, right? And this would be blackmail, not murder.

Probably disturbed by her movement, Tom woke and made the decision for her. 'What's up?' he murmured, seeing her sitting up holding her phone.

'You'll never guess.'

'Good or bad?'

'Take your pick. We didn't find *him*. *He* found *us*.'

Then followed an intense discussion, probably closer to an argument than a disagreement. Tom refused to do nothing but the safest option and Holly, crumbling with love and seeing how adorable, half awake and half naked he looked first thing in the morning fired up in protection mode, sensibly agreed. She had neither the energy nor inclination to do otherwise.

So they dressed and got down to business. Agreeing on some decisions and putting them in place before Holly borrowed Tom's ute and drove away from the farm alone.

After a rough night, deprived of her first morning coffee of the day and knowing who she was about to confront, Holly was not in the best mood. Although a respectable level of nerves battered her stomach, she also welcomed the showdown. They had all been waiting for this and it was long overdue. All being well, its success would result in celebration. Provided she could gather the evidence she needed. For reassurance, she patted the mobile in her jacket pocket. She refused to consider glitches.

He had chosen the rendezvous carefully. Secluded and isolated. Holly wondered if he had considered it also provided cover and prayed he remained a coward, without a weapon. If not, he may wave it around to threaten but she had to believe he needed money, not another life.

Forcing that thought to the front of her mind was the only way she could hold her nerve when she faced him. Responsibility and success struggled with her false bravery but she would do this. She had to. Everything depended on it.

When she arrived at the site and pulled up, he was nowhere to be seen. She had expected as much. He would be in the bush watching, casing her out.

Holly stepped from the ute, moved around to the front of it and waited out in the open. Sunrise and daybreak had already cast first light over the countryside in open paddocks but here in a sheltered clearing surrounded by thick undergrowth, Holly flinched at every shadowy movement.

Finally, he slowly emerged.

Where the hell had he been hiding this past week?

Her gaze travelled to his hands. No gun. Yet. At least, none that was visible. Unshaven. No suit. Dark casual clothes. Not quite as confident now which made him brazen and foolish enough to pull this stunt. She tensed as he moved closer.

Underneath he may be distraught but his usual surface composure remained. Except for a dangerous edge revealed in that cold stare and thin mouth.

Strained, Holly stood firm. Refused to speak first.

'You came.'

'Merely curious.'

'I would have left you alone but Fraser failed.'

Excuses. Still spineless, Holly thought.

'Your mother inherited property. Give me what I'm owed and we're done.'

Going fine so far. No sign of a weapon. Just talk. 'There is no *we*. You and I are nothing to each other. You once knew my mother, that's all.'

'Lorraine was stubborn. Didn't do her much good.' He laughed, then sobered. 'But there was always you. Half.'

Holly held his hard glare and said quietly, 'No.'

His twisted reaction was instant. The veins in his neck pulsed and his barely concealed fury boiled for release. 'You have no choice.'

His hand moved to the outside of his

coat pocket and rested there, as if in yet another warning.

A bluff. Stressed, trying to achieve all she needed, Holly said, 'I'm a waitress living in a rented cabin. Winding up an estate,' as she well knew from her legal experience, 'takes time. You seem impatient. Can you wait?'

'Then borrow it,' he hissed.

He was growing desperate. 'You don't understand. I have nothing. Even if I did, I would never hand over a cent to you.'

'You'll end up like your mother.'

Bingo. Exactly what she needed to hear. Implication. Admission of knowledge and involvement. Her gaze strayed over his shoulder to the bushland beyond. 'That sounds like a threat to me.'

'Take it any way you please. You've been warned.'

As her simmering anger grew, Holly dug deep for courage. Her words emerged in a low rasping growl. 'You may not have struck and killed my mother but you have blood on your hands. Which makes you equally guilty. No deal,' she snapped, turned and walked away.

As she hoped it would, her refusal hit his ego and arrogance. It took every ounce of restraint to continue walking and not run. She heard Porter's snarl and footsteps as he lunged forward and grabbed her from behind, flinging her about. Even as she fought against him, Holly was annoyed but calm. His fury turned to shock as they both witnessed the same thing.

The moment the meeting turned physical and he assaulted her, police and manpower burst from their concealment in the bush in every direction.

Distracted and cornered, Holly used Porter's momentary inattention to break free. In desperation, he reached for her again as a human shield but she took quick steps backward. His horrified expression recognised escape was hopeless. Stranded, he froze.

As officers caught and restrained him, Holly said quietly, 'Meet my backup.' She produced the phone in her pocket and held it up. 'Every word of our little chat was recorded.'

Porter roared like a lion, his face red and contorted.

As Norton led him away, he said to Holly, 'This is going to be one very sorry man.'

Then Tom strode toward her and gathered her fiercely in his arms. 'That went well,' she murmured, even though she was trembling.

'You should have seen the weapons and cameras trained on him.'

'Would have loved to but I was rather busy.'

'You're amazing,' he whispered.

'*Now* we can celebrate. Everything,' she sighed, before releasing years of anxiety, sinking against the warmth and protection of his body, breaking down and sobbing with relief.

Because it was close and the hub of the community, Tom drove Holly to The Coach for breakfast.

The successful arrest of Lorraine Duncan's co-conspirator killers would hit the media within hours. Until then, Holly appreciated the intimacy of the close roadhouse family. She was in a mental haze of disbelief and nervous recovery, barely coming to terms yet with how the implications of this morning's stressful encounter had now freed her life. In time, she might feel a sense of peace and closure. But for now, her mind was still processing an explosion of thoughts.

She was relieved more than happy that Fraser and Porter were caught. Trying to deal with the fact that there was no longer any need to wonder and wait. For anything. No more looking over her shoulder.

In her mind, Holly still felt adrift and detached from this new liberated existence. Comprehension had not yet fully kicked in. It was going to take a while.

The deeper reality of the senseless reason for the homicides and loss of both her parents was harder to understand, let alone accept and endure. Based on her current mood of underlying sadness and confusion, she recognised her grief would be around for the long haul. Possibly always be a part of her life. Surrounded by the love and support of her families and closest friends, she knew one day she would emerge out the other side. Perhaps more content. Just not any time soon.

'You're quiet. You okay?' Tom murmured beside her.

'I'm alive and loved. Just taking it all in.'

'Tell me what you need. I'll make it happen.'

Holly pulled a faint smile. 'Honestly, I can't answer that. I wish I knew.'

Later, Gracie took Tom aside. 'You need to take that woman away and not just for a few days. A complete break. She's been anchored to this place for years. She needs to get back out into the big wide world and start to live again.'

'Actually something came up. I have

an idea in mind.'

'Good man.' She patted his arm. 'Now take her home. I don't want to see her face around here for quite some time.'

'Be my pleasure.'

'I'm sure it already has been,' Gracie threw over her shoulder, chuckling as she wandered away. 'Just bring her back, okay?'

Tom gave her a thumbs up.

Back at Tom's farm, unpacking boxes of belongings Holly had brought from her cabin, they paused for a sundowner on the front veranda. It had become their favourite evening place. Tom with a beer, Holly a glass of wine. Taking in the stunning colours of each changing stage of sunset.

'I've been offered a long haul trucking contract.'

Holly's mood dipped a little. 'Oh?'

'Pick up a load in Melbourne. Then,' flashing her a grin, he said, 'if you're interested, I could collect you on my way back through to Adelaide and up through the Centre at Alice Springs before going on to Darwin. I'll be dropping off and reloading along the way. We could grab a break in Darwin then head south along the west coast down to Perth with a backload. Home across the Nullarbor.' He paused. 'Want to tag along?'

Holly beamed. 'Damn, yes.'

'Be roughing it for weeks and long days on outback roads?' he warned.

'I'm a country girl for life now. I'm up for it. And I'll be with you.'

Six weeks later, Tom's truck pulled up at The Coach roadhouse and he yanked his horn. Twice. Gracie dashed outside, hands on hips, beaming. Sid not far behind.

'You can see forever in this rig,' Holly said, climbing down. 'Best views of Australia.'

After lung-squeezing hugs were over, Gracie said, 'Hadn't heard from you in over a week. Wasn't sure when you were landing.'

'Top End monsoon sent us home. Plus it's almost Christmas.'

'You're looking radiant and suntanned.'

'That's because I've been travelling with my man.' Holly cleared her throat and raised her left hand.

Alice and Sophie had briefly deserted customers to join the reunion and squealed. 'You're engaged!'

'On our way through Coober Pedy on the way up.' The black opal band on her finger flashed with a row of deep blue and sea green stones.

Sid shook Tom's hand. 'Congratulations, mate.'

With arms around each other, they all walked back inside. 'So, how was your trip?'

'Wonderful,' Holly said, 'but it's so good to be home.'

ONE YEAR LATER

It had been a year for romantic commitments, Holly reflected, as she stood before the mirror in the bedroom, surrounded by her three best friends and attendants. She couldn't have chosen one. Each in their own way had come to mean so much to her so she had asked them all and they accepted. All gathered around her now in pastel floral gowns.

Addie Kendall with tiny flowers braided through her blonde hair, the new future home with Harry Chandler now built in their tree paddock. Judging by the glow on her face, eagerly anticipating her own wedding in the beautifully restored local historic *Banyandah* homestead at the end of summer.

Piper Thorne, her short dark hair with pink streaks blending perfectly with her dress, had done her own thing with Ben Powell. To be expected of such a happy independent spirit. A private ceremony, just the two of them alone together, camped deep in the Grampians Mountains where they exchanged personal commitment vows to acknowledge their promise of a lifetime partnership.

And Billie Gibbs had already married Noah Sutton in a small wedding on his farm last autumn. His daughter, Rosie, in a froth of pink and white with a tiny tiara band in her long blonde hair their lively captivating flower girl. In nostalgic memory of their first meeting again after many years, the newlyweds had honeymooned in a certain rustic shack on Reedy Lake that held special significance for them both.

So all four women now wore sparkling rings on their left hands for the men they loved, and pledged to be friends for life.

'Ready?' Billie asked Holly.

'Absolutely.'

'You've come a long way,' Piper teased.

'I remember when you were so shy,' Addie grinned.

'A special man will do that for you,' Holly agreed.

'Amen,' they all chorused.

Clutching small bunches of native wildflowers, one by one Addie, Piper and Billie escorted the bride through the house and outside, then walked ahead of Holly, following close behind, looking excitedly straight ahead at the man who had stolen her heart.

Tom turned and gazed back at her.

Even from this distance, she knew there was love in his eyes and could see the smile light up his face. The sight of him took her breath away with happiness. Waiting clean shaven and handsome in black jeans and boots, a white shirt, his black Akubra settled comfortably on his dark hair. Looking sexy and dangerous and soon to be officially hers.

Everyone turned and saw what Tom did as Holly took each step down from the veranda and walked slowly across the lawn toward the man she adored. Fresh spring flowers braided through her hair, its rusty glory tumbling over her shoulders and beyond. The gown of rich ivory had long lace sleeves, the bodice nipped in at the waist but flaring out, overlaid with lace on the maxi dress beneath. And, of course, a pair of shiny leather boots peeping out at the bottom.

A beaming Sid waited at the back row of guests and she took his arm. With humble pride, he had reluctantly agreed to give away the bride today but admitted it could not have been to a better man.

He escorted her now past the rows of families and friends. Susan Rogers like a surrogate aunt seated beside Benny Wade. Taking up two whole rows further down was her father's family. Paul and Carol Mitchell, Greg and Angela with their partners, and their children, her nephews Jack, Brady and Bobby, and niece Eva.

Across the aisle in another row, Tom's parents Allan and Meg Searle, his younger brothers Stephen and Jordan with their girlfriends all returned her smile as she passed.

All her roadhouse workmates and, in the very front row, the one and only spectacular individual so dear to her heart, stood Gracie. Shamelessly resplendent in red with strings of colourful beads around her neck and a fresh red rose in her wild piled-up crown of grey hair. Holly felt the strongest urge to stop and hug her but decided to wait and save that for later.

The ceremony was short, sweet and hilarious, Holly and Tom reciting personal individual vows of love and laughter forever.

At the end, he said, 'As long as it's legal, there's nothing I won't do for you. Just ask.'

'I'll make a list,' Holly grinned.

A wave of chuckles echoed around the guests then, before Tom kissed his bride, he threw off his hat so he could scoop his bride into his arms and concentrate on the important task.

Holly's gift to the groom was a furry bundle of Australian Shepherd sheepdog puppy with a black, tan and white coat, named *Scout*. Tom's gift to his bride was her very own farm motor bike which she couldn't wait to learn how to ride. She certainly had plenty of paddocks and back country roads to practise.

Noah Sutton's daughter, Rosie, and Tom's new puppy *Scout* were inseparable all day, romping on the grass around the farm until dark. Finally collapsing together onto the veranda seat in weary happiness, the pup with his nose tucked onto his front paws and cuddled in the little girl's arms.

Before sunset, hundreds of candles were lit, creating a dreamscape around the garden.

Dusk brought the wafting aroma of a big country barbeque to the marquee, strung with coloured lights and greenery where guests had already gathered in groups, drinking in celebration, tables beautifully laid for the meal. A spread of desserts later were made by the best country cooks in the district.

Addie Kendall was photographer for the day, capturing the essence of a couple deeply in love.

Finally, the wedding cake table was carefully wheeled out, the three-tiered piece of chocolate and artwork personally and proudly made by Sid.

Armed with a serious looking knife, Holly and Tom laid their hands over each other to cut into it and make a wish. While that was being served out, a local band started up, playing a slow country waltz, enticing the bride and groom into each other's arms and onto the floor.

'Can you dance?' Holly asked.

'Some,' Tom murmured. 'If we hold onto each other, we'll be fine.'

Later, fireworks were lit by the reedy dam. Holly and Tom, arms around each other, strolled closer down the hill with everyone, some bare foot, some in boots, to watch the explosion of colour and noise.

Everyone was smiling, all with their own special memories of a memorable occasion.

'Best day ever or what?' she whispered.

He nodded. 'And plenty more to come. I promise.'